The Prisoners of Stewartville

The Prisoners
of Stewartville

by
Shannon Felton

Cover illustration and design by Kealan Patrick Burke
www.elderlemondesign.net

First Brigids Gate Press Edition: June 2022
First Edition printed by Silver Shamrock Press: February 2020

ISBN (paperback): 978-1-957537-31-3
ISBN (Kindle ebook): 978-1-957537-30-6
Library of Congress Control Number: 2022941547

BRIGIDS GATE PRESS
Bucyrus, Kansas
www.brigidsgatepress.com

Printed in the United States of America

This book is dedicated to my husband, Ben, whose love makes all things possible.

Special Thanks to Meredith Lozaga and Kim Arntsen, as well as the amazing writers of RDR, for the incredible help and support they provided.

Content warnings are provided at the end of this book.

BRICKS

Chapter One

People moved to Stewartville for three reasons and three reasons only: they worked for the prisons, they had family in the prisons, or they were in prison. Growing up, that meant I didn't know a single kid whose parent wasn't either a prison guard or an inmate. And if you thought there was a big difference between the two, you'd be wrong.

Take Denny's mom, for example.

We were sitting in his basement playing Mortal Kombat when she banged open the door at the top of the stairs. She was still wearing her olive green prison uniform; her face red and her neck popping with veins. Out of nowhere she threw her work boot down and hit Denny in the back of the head, which really must have hurt because they were steel-toe.

"You got a fucking 'D' in history?" she shouted. "*And* you didn't do the dishes? *And* it smells like fucking pot down here. I can't keep *doing* this with you! I can't!" Another boot came flying down the stairs, but luckily it veered right and hit the brick wall instead of our skulls. "I've had it! I swear to God, I've fucking had it! *What the fuck is wrong with you?*"

Denny didn't answer. He just kept his eyes locked on the screen while his cheeks turned a splotchy red. I could feel the humiliation and anger radiating off him like a heat lamp.

"You're turning into nothing but a fat fucking loser, I hope you know that," she said. "Bring me that god damn Sega and send your friend home. You're grounded until your grades go up." She slammed the door, and we listened as her footsteps stomped overhead.

I shot Denny a look from the corner of my eye but kept my mouth shut. He was a chubby kid ("husky" according to his Wrangler jeans), and his T-shirts were always a size too small so they'd pull tight at his gut. He'd just moved into town a few weeks ago, but he was a funny guy and he seemed cool enough.

A door upstairs opened and closed and the footsteps stopped. Denny let out a breath.

"Sorry about my mom," he said.

I shrugged. "Don't worry about it."

"She didn't use to be like that." He lifted a hand up to where the boot had hit. "She's just changed since we moved here."

"Yeah, this place does that—turns people into assholes."

I'd seen it plenty of times. Nice, normal families transferring in from Mayberry, USA—where prison was just another job in a great big world—suddenly being stuck in the stifling grimy bubble of Stewartville, Fifth Layer of Hell, where prison was the center of life. I mean, deep down I got it. Mom and Dad work with inmates all day, getting literal shit or bloody tampons thrown on them, wrestling down some nut job who thinks the devil is in his eyeballs and has just blinded himself with a plastic fork, and all they can probably think coming home is god forbid *their* kid becomes the disgusting slob hiding Twinkies between his fat rolls in an eight-by-eight cell.

And it wasn't like they could get away from it and gain some perspective, either. Nope. No matter where they went—the grocery store, the doctor's office, their kid's school—there were always guards off work but still dressed in their uniforms, always a DOC bus driving by them on the road, and usually always a siren or two going off somewhere in town.

And so Denny's mom had her nerves frayed thin. She'd probably been dealing with inmates who acted like three-year-olds all day, was sick and tired of people who refused to take personal accountability and who had ruined their lives, and she'd come home and lost it. It's still fucked up no matter what.

"Yeah, well, I guess I better take this up to her," Denny said. He pushed himself off the couch and went over to TV. I set the controller down on the makeshift coffee table — just two milk crates and an old board — and pretended not to see him wiping at his eyes.

Together we moved the entertainment stand away from the wall, and while Denny hiked up his jeans and got to work disconnecting the wires, I crouched down and picked up his mom's boot.

"Damn," I said. "She threw this shit so hard she knocked a fucking brick out."

The painted wall opposite the stairs was peeling around the cracks and in the middle, where the boot had hit, was a black hole.

I put my hand up to the wall. Air whistled against my fingertips, cool and damp.

"Huh," I said. "There's a draft coming through here."

Denny looked over at me as he wrapped the wires around his palm. "You think something's back there?"

"I don't know." I bent my head down and peered in, expecting to see some boarding or framing, but instead it was pitch black. "Seems like it."

Denny set the wires down and squatted next to me and I scooted over so he could look in too. "Let me see your lighter," he said.

I dug into my flannel pocket and gave it to him. He stuck his hand in the hole—*Watch something bite it off,* he joked— lit the lighter, then bent his neck forward and peered through the slot.

"Yeah, dude, I think there's a freaking *tunnel* back there," he said.

"Please tell me you're joking."

He got down on his knees and wiggled the corners of the top brick loose. After a few tugs it gently slid out of the wall. Then he did the same with three more.

He flicked the lighter again and held the flame up to the hole. We put our heads together and peered in. Sure enough, rounded dirt walls lead back into a circle of darkness.

"Nope. No joke," he said.

I moved my head away from his hand before he caught my eyebrows on fire. "Holy shit, dude."

Denny pulled his hand out. "Well, this house *is* old as shit, right?" he asked.

"Yeah, probably."

"So it could be anything. Maybe there's a room or something back there. Maybe it goes to the prisons." His face brightened. "We should check it out."

"Uh, *fuck that.*" I was sure that any room that required a secret tunnel blocked off by a brick wall was the last thing we needed to check out.

"Oh, come on, dude. Don't be such a pussy," he said.

I stood up, claustrophobia tightening my chest. "Man, I'm serious. You should probably leave that alone. Put the bricks back," I said.

"No way. I want to find out where this goes." He peered back into the hole and then tried to wiggle another brick loose. It came out of the wall and the basement seemed to shrink with it, the bricks and wooden beams closing in on us, the shadows stretching, the black hole slowly sucking the room into it, millimeter by millimeter.

A door slammed upstairs. Denny and I flinched and stared up at the ceiling, waiting for the sound of approaching footsteps.

"Hey man, I should probably get out of here," I said, happy for the excuse to leave. I pushed myself upright and stuck my hands in my pockets. "Your skull gonna be all right?"

Denny put a hand up to his brown curls. "Yeah, I'll be fine," he said. "Hard-headed." He'd tried to make a joke, but his cheeks had become splotchy again.

"All right, man." I hung back a minute more, feeling guilty for taking off on him, but not really wanting to stick around any longer than I had to either. "Well. I guess I'll catch you at school tomorrow. And leave that shit alone."

He nodded and flashed me a peace sign. I started up the rickety wooden stairs and turned back to see him replacing the bricks. Then he bent down and finished gathering up his game system and carefully, slowly, I opened the door to the kitchen. The last thing I wanted to do was run into Denny's mom again. But the house was quiet, and I made it to the backdoor just as Denny's grandpa started hacking up a lung upstairs.

I hurried out onto the back steps, shut the door softly, and glanced up through the panes just as the latch caught.

Denny's mom was standing in the dark hallway right off the kitchen. I held my breath and waited for her eyes to turn my way, for her face to go red and her neck veins to pop, but she kept staring at the wall, arms dangling at her sides.

And then she dropped her head in her hands and began to cry.

"Fuckin A," I whispered. I turned down the steps, ducked under the clothesline, and looked back over my shoulder once I hit the alley.

Denny was right, from the looks of things his house must have been sitting there for at least a century. It wasn't anything special, just an old white clapboard with black trim sitting on the corner. But I still had a bad feeling. That wasn't unusual for Stewartville, the holy fucking Mecca of bad feelings, but this was different.

Chapter Two

It was a three cigarette walk home from Denny's to the Shady Acres trailer park, situated right on the south edge of town with nothing across the road but an expanse of flat land that broke up at the horizon by concrete compounds. At night, the prisons were islands of orange lights in a sea of black, and when I laid in bed, the glow of them washed over the ceiling and down the wall. In the quiet I could hear the far-off hum of their mechanizations and I'd think about my mom, out there in the beast's belly.

Ours was the first trailer to the right of the entrance so we at least had the row of overhanging trees from the street to beautify our particular lot, and I'd always liked how the brown of our siding blended in nicely with the wood. Not that it wasn't still a shit hole, because it was. But you got to take what you can get.

I stomped up the warped wooden deck—past the old coffee cans, aquariums and cracked storage bins—and pulled open the screen door so I could push open the dented aluminum one behind it. Shane was waiting in the living room, sitting on the orange floral couch that we'd had forever, pulling on his boots. He worked nights over at the cement plant and if there was any place in Stewartville that looked more depressing than the prisons, that was it.

I'd gone to help him once, to earn a little under the table pay. He worked in a small side building out in the scrubs, with no A/C, and all we did all day was walk around in a circle for a while, holding long white tubes, which we had to hit against the ground with every step to pack the powder inside. The whole time all I could think about was giant cigarettes and so the minutes dragged on until that first smoke break. Then I learned there was no smoking allowed. Explosives, and flammables, and bears oh my. Didn't that just figure. I never went back, and he never asked why.

"Where you been?" he asked.

"Out."

"Out where?"

"A friend's, man. Chill."

He grabbed his work shirt off the arm of the sofa and shrugged it on over his wife beater, eyeing me down as he buttoned it up, bottom to top. "Watch the attitude, little dude. And make sure you eat something and get your homework done."

"What's for dinner?"

"Hot dogs." The lucky bastard had gotten all the looks in the family—probably because we had different dads, and his wasn't a meth head that mom had hooked up with on a bender—but he was still a shit cook.

See, Shane and I made a pact back when I was in eighth grade, on the afternoon when mom's probation officer had come by the trailer to give us the news that she was going back to lock up. And after sitting round the living room for a bit—the both of us trying our best not to cry—Shane had driven me south out of town, past the prisons and decrepit old trailers, up to where the world always seemed like a speck of dust beneath the sun.

Skull Rock looked exactly like its name and we'd walked over to it across dry, caked dirt littered with beer cans and cigarette butts and climbed up to our seats atop it. It wasn't the best view, but looking down on the prisons for a change sure beat looking forward to them, you know?

Because it always seemed to me that if you lived in Stewartville, you eventually ended up in prison. It was as if there was a fork in the road and you could either go left and work at the prison or you could go right and get sentenced to one. Wasn't much of a difference though, if you asked me. Not in Stewartville.

And you'd think you could tell who would be who, right? But you'd be surprised. Your sexy, shy, straight-A babysitter from last year would be a ninety-one-pound junkie—teeth rotting from her head, skin grey, her blonde hair thinning into nasty ass clumps— the next. And then she'd be gone, except to maybe pop up in the *Stewartville Herald* police record once in a while, wearing an old Mickey Mouse T-shirt, busted for robbery or aggravated assault, or whatever the hell else she had done for some cash.

"Listen, little dude," Shane had said, taking a hit off a joint and passing it to me. "Don't mess with any man-made stuff, okay? Just the God-given shit."

"Like what?" I'd asked, taking a hit and trying not to embarrass myself by coughing.

"Like weed? Shrooms? That shits cool. That shit grows natural, you know? But not the synthetic stuff. Meth, heroin, that's the devil's shit."

I shrugged. "Sure," I'd said. I didn't even like getting fucked up that much. Made me think about shit I didn't want to be thinking about. Like mom.

"I'm not kidding, bro. That shit will eat your soul. You got to promise me."

I looked down on Stewartville, with its faded houses and concrete prison yards, and I'd nodded. "You too?" I'd asked.

"For sure, bro." He'd taken the joint back from me and held up his fist to my own. "We're gonna be fine. I promise."

Boom. Done.

I don't know if hot dogs were what you'd call fine, but the pot was sitting out on the stove so I dipped two fingers into the cold water and grabbed one of the congealed beef sticks.

"Hey. Get a fork and plate, dipshit. I'm tired of cleaning up after you."

"All right, all right. Relax." I opened the cabinet overhead, pulled a plate down, and waved it at him as evidence of my obedience.

"Mom wrote," he said.

"Yay." I set the plate down and opened the drawer for a fork.

"And talk to Nana before you go to bed." He grabbed his keys off the hook. "She's had a hard day."

I nodded, only because there was a wad of cow assholes in my cheek to keep me from being a smart ass, and as soon as the door shut behind him I put the clean plate back into the cabinet. I grabbed the last two hot dogs from the pot, stuffed the envelope in my back pocket, and then made my way back through the living room and down the narrow hall to check on Nana.

I knocked on the door, one of those hollow particle board ones, then pushed it open just slightly. Nana was laying in bed under the glow of her bedside lamp, curled up beneath her pink ruffled comforter with her sleeping bonnet on. She had soaps on the TV, reruns playing on an old recorded tape that she hadn't taken out of the VCR in decades.

"Hey, Nana. Everything going all right?"

She turned to look at me and that's when I knew something was wrong. Nana didn't drag her eyes away from her soaps for any ole thing. Her bottom lip began to tremble. "They took her head."

I took a bite of my hot dog and leaned against the door frame. "What's that?"

"Betty's *head*. They took it." She lifted her tiny wrinkled hands and pet the sides of her cheeks.

"Who did?"

"Those *people*." She waved an agitated hand at her nightstand. I stepped into the room, usually a big no-no because of all the things she had hoarded everywhere, and took the brochure that was laying under the old Chantilly lamp next to the TV Guide.

Frazier Medical Research and Scientific Development

Oh, right. I flipped the brochure back onto the nightstand. "Nana, Betty agreed to donate her body. For science. So they'd pay her funeral costs."

Nana scoffed and spit air in annoyance. "I don't care. And I'm sure she didn't agree to her head being out there in the world somewhere." She waved her hand in the air and I got a visual of Betty's head "out there somewhere", touring Paris and sending us postcards.

"And just what do they need her head for, anyhow?" Nana asked. "Ain't nobody would want a brain transplant from *Betty*."

I tried not to laugh. It was morbid and awful, and also a little funny. But I put on a serious face and stopped myself from taking another bite of my hot dog. Out of respect and all.

"Nobody's *getting* Betty's brain, Nana. They're just going to use it for studies. And it was a good thing for her and her family. You know she didn't have money for a funeral."

But that just made Nana's bottom lip tremble and the tears well up in her eyes. "Well, I already signed with them too," she whimpered. "But I didn't know they'd want my head."

I sighed and stepped all the way into the room, sitting down on the edge of the bed. I held one hotdog in the hand resting in my lap, and the other wiggled back and forth in the hand that patted her shoulder.

"I can just picture her head sitting out on a tray, her dead eyes open and staring at nothing," she wailed. And I had to admit, it was definitely a more depressing idea than Paris. "Oh, it's awful. Just awful!" She looked up at me and clutched my arm. "Don't let them do that to me."

"It'll be fine, Nana. I won't let them take your head."

She let go of my arm and laid back on the pillow. "You promise?"

"I promise."

"You're a good child, honey." She sniffled and waved a hand at me. "You go on to bed now and let me watch my stories."

"All right, Nana." I rose and went to the door, turning back as an afterthought. "Shane give you your pills?"

"Yessir, he did."

"Night then."

I shut the door. I didn't have far to go to get to my room, I just had to stick my right hand out and turn the knob that was there. Trailers aren't exactly roomy. My bedroom door wouldn't even open all the way, not with my mattress blocking it, so I sidled through the crack, climbing onto the bed with my knees, and then pushed the door shut with my foot.

I pulled the envelope out of my pocket and looked at the address. *Unit 4.* They moved her. It didn't matter. Here or there, it still wasn't home. I tossed it unread in the box with the rest.

Chapter Three

You wouldn't know it from the looks of things, but there was big money in the prison industry. State funding, federal funding, you name it. But all that money? It just went right back into the prison system. State-of-the-art *everything*. Security, weight rooms, computerized systems, whatever. Meanwhile, the high school was slowly sinking into the landfill they had built it on while the students inside recorded audiobooks for the inmate literacy program. That's how I had met Denny.

We were both assigned to ROTC for the last block, but I guess there was something about us that didn't look like the shootin' and salutin' type. So the drill instructor sent us down to the small A/V room instead, where we sat at a little table between wooden shelving and rolling TV stands, with a stack of kids' books and a tape recorder in front of us. After we recorded a book, we put both it and the tape in a Ziploc baggie, marked it, and then put the baggie in a box that went out every couple of weeks.

The room itself was under both the auditorium stage and Ms. Alvarez's office, cut off from the rest of the school. Which was honestly a nice break from all the drama and chaos, but sometimes it'd get so quiet in there that when we weren't recording, all we could hear was the fluorescent light buzzing above us. I didn't like the quiet too much. Made the room feel smaller. Darker.

Denny was waiting when I got there the next day, and shortly after that Ms. Alvarez came in to make sure we were present.

"Don't mind me, boys," she said. "I just need to find some props for the drama class." She walked to the end shelf and bent over the boxes, her red skirt pulling tight across her ass. Denny and I glanced at each other and sat up a little straighter. Rumor was that she had a thing going with the varsity football players, and we didn't much mind her maybe taking notice of us too.

No such luck. I pulled the box of books closer and started looking through them.

Most of the books were early chapter readers and Denny and I had gotten pretty bored with them after the first two weeks. So we'd started to fuck around with the character voices—adding in dramatic sound effects in the background, the opening and closing of doors, footsteps—all that jazz. We had fun with it. About as much as we could, anyway.

By the time we finished the second book Ms. Alvarez had left and class was almost over. I hit stop on the recorder and glanced up at the clock. "No point starting another," I said. "We only got, like, fifteen minutes left."

Denny took the book and turned it over in his hands. "So about that tunnel."

"Man…" I reached into my jeans, pulled out my lighter, and tapped it against the tabletop. Spin, tap. Spin, tap. It was a nervous habit of mine, mostly when I wanted a smoke and couldn't have one. I'd tried chew once, just to cut the cravings at school, but on my first try, I'd swallowed some spit and threw up all over my shoes. That and I didn't want nasty teeth. "You need to just leave that shit alone and stay out of there," I said.

"No way, dude. It's cool as hell."

"You didn't go in already, did you?" I asked.

"Nah, dude." He set the book down. "Thought about it though."

"Bad idea, man. Honestly, I don't even know how you can sleep down there knowing that thing is in your wall."

He smiled, leaned back, and rested an arm on the back of his chair. "Why's that? You afraid of ghosts?"

"Get real." I spun the lighter—spin-tap, spin-tap—on the cool laminated wood. "What I *mean* is, it's probably not safe. Structurally, you know?"

His smile turned into a grin. "That's bullshit. You're just a little pussy, admit it."

"Man, fuck off."

The tape recorder between us clicked, and we both looked down at the same time.

"Huh," I said. "I guess the stop button got stuck."

Denny reached a hand forward, hit rewind for a quick second, then played the tape.

So I've been thinking about that tunnel.
You didn't go in, did you?
Nah, man. Thought about it, though.
Bad idea, dude.

Denny hit stop. "Well, that was spooky as shit," he said. He dropped his chair forward and leaned towards the recorder. "Guess maybe we should do something else if we're pissing off your ghosts." He bounced between hitting rewind and play a few times until he'd found a spot close to the end of the book.

"What are you doing?" I asked.

"I wanna do some skits."

I groaned. "Not this shit again."

"Come on, man. It'll be fun."

Denny liked to think he was a comedian and to be fair, I had to give him props for cracking me up. But I was just some lame ass kid sitting in the high school basement with nothing better to do but to laugh at his corny jokes, so it wasn't like I was the best judge or anything.

"We'll do it like a radio show." He waved a hand at the look I imagine was on my face. "You'll see."

We sat there and waited for the story to end, and I cringed at the sound of my voice, made even worse because I was talking like a dog. (*Why, I doooo know where your booooone is, Mr. Snuffles. Woof-woof.*) When we finished, he stopped the playback and then pushed record once more.

A few seconds of dead air ran and for the briefest moment I thought I heard something. "Hey, did you—"

He held up a finger for me to wait. And then he spoke. "*Greetings,* Prisoners of Stewartville. This is KUNT FM, bringing you the best of radio talk live. I'm your host, Johnny Grabadick, and with me today is Adam Suckanipple. How are you today, Mr. Suckanipple?"

He raised his eyebrows and waited. I cleared my throat and leaned forward closer to the mic. "I'm good, Johnny. Thanks."

"Fan-fucking-tastic! Though I guess anything beats being in prison, am

I right?"

I laughed. Couldn't help myself. "That's right, Johnny."

"No offense to our audience, of course."

"Hey, *they're* the offenders here, Grabadick."

"That they are, Suckanipple. That they are."

"Just a little light-hearted teasing," I said, appealing to the understanding listeners on tape.

"You know what my daddy always said, 'If you ain't got a sense of humor, you ain't got nuttin'.'"

"Did he really say that?"

"Oh, *fuck* no." Denny laughed, as harshly as he should have. "He was a fucking miserable drunk that treated my mom like crap."

The moment almost got heavy, so I leaned closer to the mic.

"Remember kids, always respect your elders," I joked.

"Yeah," Denny laughed. "*That's* why they're in there."

See? Corny. But we cracked ourselves up until the dismissal bell rang, anyway.

"Aren't you gonna erase it?" I asked as we stood and grabbed our bags.

"Nah. Just gonna rewind it to the beginning." He hit the button, waited, then slid the book and the tape in the Ziploc baggie.

"What's the point of that?" I asked as he dropped it in the box.

"I just think it would be kinda cool, you know?"

We headed through the auditorium and out into the halls.

"What would?"

"If the prisoners liked our skits and started requesting us to do the tapes."

Look, not that it wasn't fun killing some time with Denny, but it wasn't like I cared if the inmates liked the tapes or not. It left me with an eerie feeling, thinking about some prisoner listening to my voice alone in his cell. It was too close for comfort. Too *intimate*. Like I was right there with him.

"That's fucking dumb, man," I said. "Besides, they're just gonna turn the tape off at the end of the book, anyway. No one's ever gonna hear that shit."

"It's not dumb, dude. Johnny Cash played at Folsom."

I laughed. "What the fuck does that have to do with anything? And really? You're fucking Johnny Cash now?"

His cheeks splotched up. "I'm just saying, entertainers perform for prisoners all the time. And hey," his face cracked into another grin, "maybe you'll catch one of my shows when you're in there."

"Man, fuck off."

"No, *you* fuck off."

We stepped through the double doors and out onto the steps, squinting against the glare of the sun.

"So you coming over or what?" he asked.

I dug into my pockets, lit a cigarette, exhaled. "Aren't you grounded?" I asked.

"Nah, she felt bad for overreacting." He fanned the smoke away from his face. "Come on. I wanna check out that tunnel."

"I don't know, man."

"Dude, I promise. We'll just go in a little ways and see what's down there." He took a step down, as if we had already decided. "I'm not asking you to go spelunking or anything."

"What about your mom?"

"Don't even worry about that. She's at work. Come on. If you do this, I promise I'll let you get that Scorpion fatality next time we play."

I took a drag. Scoffed. "Fine, whatever. Fuck it."

He smiled and his dimples popped. "That's the spirit."

Chapter Four

We walked down the gravel shoulder of the highway for about two blocks, coming up on a *Caution: Inmates Working* sign put on the side of the road by the old, two pump gas station.

"Know any of them?" Denny asked. We eyed the prisoners pulling weeds and picking trash in the median. They were in your classic black-and-white striped uniforms, bright orange road vests on over that, and they turned their heads and watched us as we walked along.

I nodded at Denny. "Yeah, I know a few of them."

Of course the dumbass waved. And naturally, a few of the mofos across the road waved back.

"Hey, sweet thangs!" one of them yelled. Then it was laughing and catcalls all the way down the line until a guard came along and shut that shit down.

I shrugged at Denny's blush. "You get what you ask for, dumbass."

We were all jokes the rest of the way, right up to when we walked through his front door and realized we weren't alone.

Denny's mom came out of the kitchen and looked us up and down as she carefully dried her hands on a dishcloth.

"Oh. Hey, Mom." Denny dropped his bag by the door and gave me a sideways glance.

"You didn't tell me you were having company today," she said.

"I thought you'd—I mean. Yeah, we're just making a quick pit stop before heading back out."

"I see." But her sour expression didn't change, and she just kept staring me down, wiping that cloth along one hand to the next. "I'm sorry. I didn't catch your name last time."

I didn't want to tell her. It was a gut thing, and I always trusted my gut. It'd gotten me out of trouble more times than I could count, to the point I'd started to think I was developing a sixth sense for when cops were around.

So I lied. "James Hetfield."

Thank god she wasn't familiar with Metallica. "Hetfield," she repeated. "Your mother wouldn't be over at Women's would she, James?"

"Mom!" Denny's splotches made another appearance.

"Well?" she asked again.

So I lied again. "No, ma'am."

"Hm." She flipped the dish towel over her shoulder. "We have an inmate over there that looks a lot like you. Same coloring and eyes."

Denny finally found his balls. "Geez Louise, Mom. You can't just ask that kind of stuff." He nudged me. "Sorry, man. You wanna juice or something before we take off?"

"Sure, but I gotta pi—uh, use the restroom first."

"Upstairs, first door on the left," his mom said. "Keep it down and stay out of the bedrooms."

"Thank you. Yes, ma'am." I passed by the stacks of boxes that still lined the bare white walls and Denny's voice trailed off as they went into the kitchen.

"... what is wrong with you? You can't just do that, Mom."

I let out a deep breath as I climbed the stairs, *trying* to be as quiet as possible, but my footsteps still echoed on the hollow, wooden steps. At the top, a door stood open at the end of the hall and thin sunlight streamed through the room's foggy window onto the edge of a mattress. Upon the mattress was an arm. Bony and unmoving.

The floorboards creaked as I made my way to the bathroom and the arm bent at the elbow, pushing its body up. I ducked into the bathroom before Denny's grandpa could call out to me.

But he was waiting, and he caught me on the exit.

"Hey. Hey you." His voice was dry and raspy and desperate.

I stopped, hand on the bathroom knob, and looked in. The old man was sitting up against the pillows, wearing a thin, brown polyester shirt that made his collar bone look like a wire hanger.

"Come here for a second," he said.

"I just needed to use the—"

He interrupted me with his hacking, phlegmy cough.

"Just come here, you little shit," he wheezed.

I exhaled and took a few steps closer, stopping just inside the doorway.

The room was large, and bare, and depressing, containing only the small iron bed he was lying on and a dresser opposite of that.

"Get the remote for me," he said, pointing at the dresser.

Denny's mom would probably kill me for going in, but the remote was laying right there in front of the TV. I stepped in, and as soon as I did, I felt the emptiness. But it was an emptiness full of meaning, like a graveyard, you know?

Anyway, I crossed the room, grabbed the remote off the stand, and brought it over to him.

He took it in his left hand and his long, yellowed nails lightly scratched across my wrist. Then he motioned for me to come closer with his right.

I leaned in, noticing how the blunt silver needles in his stubble caught the light.

"You got a cigarette?" he whispered through dry, cracked lips.

"Um…"

His hand shot out and grabbed onto my jacket, and he pulled me down even closer to his rotted teeth and bloodshot eyes.

"Come on, now. Just a drag."

"Sorry. I don't—"

He yanked on my jacket again and I almost fell down on top of him. I'm sure if that had happened his bones would have crunched beneath me like a pile of eggshells.

"I can smell it on you, you little asshole."

His breath fluttered against my hair, that's how close I was. I could smell him— the BO, the bad breath, the musk of passing and aging time—and I tried to pull away. But he held on tight and I dragged his upper body along to the edge of the mattress.

"Fucking A," I said as he clung onto me. The sheet had slid from his lower half, revealing his tighty-whities—stained at the crotch with little yellow droplets of piss—and the straps over his pale bony legs, chafing the skin and keeping him bound to the mattress.

"Jesus Christ. Here." I reached into my pocket and pulled out the cigarettes. His fingers went flying, bony and frantic grasshoppers, a biblical plague of addiction, and they clenched and grasped so spastically at the pack they crushed half of the cigarettes.

The poor bastard's hand trembled as he pulled a smoke out and brought it to his lips. When he opened his mouth strings of saliva spread between his coated teeth and I glanced around for a glass of water in the bare room.

"Light it," he whispered. Desperate. Tears in his eyes. "Hurry."

I flicked the lighter and held it out for him. He sucked on the filter, smacking his lips against it like a fish wanting air, then he inhaled, exhaled, and fell back against the pillows.

"God *damn*, that's good," he sighed. It brought a half-smile to my lips.

But then I looked over my shoulder, knowing how much time had passed, and I definitely didn't want Denny's mom catching me there.

"Listen man, I should probably get downstairs," I said.

His eyes widened and crossed as he looked down at the cig and took another drag. "Watch out for them down there," he said, speaking around the filter.

"Who? Ms. Duncan?"

The air in the room got heavier as the smoke settled into a cloudy haze.

"I can hear 'em in the walls," he said. He took another drag and closed his eyes. "Them's what made me sick."

I waited for him to explain, knowing from experience that you couldn't rush these things, that you got to let their delusions unravel for you slowly. But he wasn't interested in saying anything else. He opened his eyes again, pulled the cigarette away from his lips, and handed it to me.

"Drop that in the toilet," he said.

I took it and pulled the sheet back over his legs before heading to the door.

"Hey. Hey you," he called out, just as I made it back into the hall.

I looked back over my shoulder.

"You got a cigarette?"

Chapter Five

"Well, that's a fucking bummer," Denny said. Since his mom was home, we bailed and headed downtown. There we were walking, him sucking on a juice pouch and me sucking on a cigarette. "I really wanted to check out that tunnel," he complained.

"Maybe next time, man."

"Yeah, right. You barely wanted to this time. Seriously, how are you not fucking curious, dude?"

I shrugged. "It's either just a dead-end tunnel or it's something fucked up."

"Wow. Such an optimist."

"Come on, man, get real," I said. "This is Stewartville. What do you think's gonna be in there? A pot of gold?"

"Why the hell not, pussy?"

I stuck my foot out and hit the soles of his shoes so he'd stumble, which he did.

"You fucker," he said.

"Hey, Denny, I forgot to ask. Your momma sell potato chips?"

"What?"

"I'm just saying, I saw her on the street corner yesterday with a sign that said 'Lays: Twenty-five cents.'"

"Oh, you're a cocksucker." He threw his empty juice packet at me. "Look at who's got the jokes now."

I laughed and dodged the pouch, then kicked it from the sidewalk where it had landed in front of me. "That's what you get for calling me a pussy," I said.

"So why'd you lie to her, dude? About your name?"

I took a drag. "I don't know, man. Just seemed best that way." Because when your moms on the inside and you're dealing with her guards on the outside, anything you say or do can and will be held against her in the penitentiary. Meaning you don't want to draw any attention to her, you know? Piss off the wrong person *out here* and she might stop getting her mail *in there*, or her commissary will come up short, or she'll wind up alone in a room with the wrong person. Nah, staying out of shit was best.

"Sorry again about how weird she was," Denny said. "Seriously, dude, she was always a pain, but she's gotten so much worse. It's like she's not even herself anymore."

"I told you, this place—"

"What if it's that tunnel?" He stopped walking and shoved his hands deep in his pockets.

I took a drag and looked him over. "You're serious?"

He nodded, kicked a rock, and resumed walking.

"Why would the tunnel make her worse?" I asked.

"I don't know, like we let out bad vibes or something."

"I mean, she wasn't that great before we found the tunnel." I glanced over, worried I'd crossed a line. "No offense."

"Yeah, I know. But I'm telling you, it's worse." The splotches on his cheeks came back, and I got the feeling he wanted to drop it. So I asked no more questions about his mom, but I was curious about something else.

"If you think it's so bad, then why in the fuck would you want to go in there, man?"

"I didn't think about it until just now." He gave me a sheepish grin, one dimple popping. "I guess I sound pretty crazy, right?"

I laughed and took a drag. "I don't know, maybe it's toxic mold."

He laughed, which I was happy to hear. "Yeah, maybe."

By the time we walked the last three blocks the sun had set, and the cars were cruising the strip—their lights flooding the road in yellows and reds—and in the dark alcoves of abandoned storefronts kids were already sneaking shots and hits. See, Stewartville didn't have a movie theater let alone the internet, so we mostly entertained ourselves with sex, drugs, and rock 'n' roll. The classic small town epidemic, right? And the best place to go for all that—the only place really—was Comet's Arcade.

Every evening, two-thirds of the student population descended upon Comet's and spilled out onto the sidewalk in swarming crowds that loitered in front of the pawnshops and bars. Because even though Comet's was the hub of downtown, it was still just one more shitty hole-in-the-wall place. Long and narrow, the room contained two pool tables, some booths along both walls, one actual, legit video game that no one ever played, and a jukebox. No, what Comet's *really* had to offer was frozen burritos, music, a public restroom, and a central place to connect with some weed and liquor. All in the shadow of Old Max, down at the end of Main.

If you were a stoner or a freak you stayed on the north side of Main. Because across the street, in the dirt lot alongside the old pharmacy, was where the shitkickers went to park their pickup trucks and drink their whiskey, and no one wanted to hang with those dudes.

They were pretty wasted over there by the time Denny and I showed up, hooting and hollering and playing their country music loud enough to drown out the jukebox from Comet's, pissing off everyone else across the road just like they wanted.

"Redneck fucks!" a kid yelled at them as he cruised by slowly in his Ford Taurus. A beer bottle went flying out the driver side window and shattered beneath the tailgate of the nearest truck and a flock of cowboy hats rushed out into the street. The driver hit the gas and peeled around the corner, but he'd be back around for another cruise and inevitably a fight would break out between both sides of the road. Like this was all some kind of nightly reenactment of *West Side Story*.

Which sounds old-fashioned, but time was funny like that in Stewartville. Probably because of all the ex-cons walking around who acted like it was still the year they went in the can.

Zeke spotted us a few doors down from Comet's and shook a bottle of Jim Beam up in the air, looking like he'd just won the Superbowl and had gotten his trophy. "Yo, bro!" he called. "Come and get some of this."

So Denny and I followed his bouncing blonde Chia Pet braids while he grabbed more people to come join us in the alley. By the time we got back there, there were so many people with us we all only got a shot or two each, but that's just how Zeke was.

We'd known each other since forever. His mom had graduated here and then had gotten a job as a guard over at one of the men's facilities. She'd been a cool lady, always asking about school and giving me advice and shit. She'd give you the shirt right off her back, same as Zeke. Which for him was usually a Rastafarian Frog tee. But then she'd fallen for an inmate she'd gone to school with—got caught sneaking him into secure areas, sneaking him contraband—and that had earned her a four-year sentence over at Women's.

It was a crowd of us that stood in a circle, bull-shitting in the dark just outside of the streetlights, and I introduced Denny to the motley crew as the bottle went around: *Hey, dude, meet two-finger Ryan, meet Craig the midget.* And so on.

Eventually the crowd broke up to either find more mood enhancing substances or to go suck and fuck behind the dumpsters, and Denny and I sat our asses down against Comet's back wall. Charlie joined us and pulled out a baggie. Zeke wandered over to a window well to smash his empty bottle.

Charlie was kind of a trip. For starters, he was brown from head to toe—dreadlocks, ruddy skin, baggy clothes, eyes—all of it brown. And because of the patchouli oil he wore, he even *smelled* brown, like old bread and fertilized dirt. He was in his forties and had fought in Vietnam, but what he was notorious for around town was dropping twenty-three tabs of acid at his mother's funeral. My mom had hung out with him for a while, back when she still spent most of her energy getting prettied up for her nightly trips to the bar instead of letting her teeth rot out for meth, and I was sure he'd always had a crush on her.

"So what have you been up to, man?" he asked me.

I shrugged and pulled out a smoke. "Nothing much. Hanging out with Denny here. He's new to town."

Charlie slapped him on the knee. "Oh yeah, man? So whaddya think of it so far?" He sprinkled some herb in the bowl and packed it with his thumb.

Denny leaned forward over his criss-crossed applesauced legs and shrugged as Zeke came back over. "It's all right, I guess."

"Pfft. You ain't been here long enough then," Zeke said. He sat down and took the pipe from Charlie. "This place'll get to you after a while." The sticks and seeds crackled beneath the lighter as he took a hit. "It gets to everyone eventually," he said, exhaling and coughing.

"Oh yeah, man," Charlie took the pipe back and handed it over to Denny. "It's because of the ley lines."

"Ley lines?" Denny asked, bending his head down to the pipe. The lighter lit up his face and the puddles of condensation along the wall glittered with reflected flame.

"Don't listen to him," I said, winking at Charlie. "It's just his hippie shit."

Charlie nudged Denny to get his attention back and continued. "Nah man, for real, check it out. Ley lines are these energy vibrations that run through the earth, right, man? Like at the Bermuda Triangle. And they all converge right here in Stewartville, creating a vortex of weird." He used both hands to draw a bubble in the air, punctuating his words like some kind of mystical shaman.

Zeke laughed and kicked my shoe. "'Vortex of weird.'"

At the ends of the alley, groups of people walked by laughing and hollering, and the cars kept cruising.

"I'm not kidding, man." Charlie leaned back and wrapped his arms around his knees. "It's the reason all this bad shit happens here. I seen it when I was tripping out on Dobson Road. All these blue lines leading right into town, dude."

Charlie was always seeing shit. Twenty-three hits of acid will do that to you, I guess. But Denny ate that shit up.

"Like what kind of bad stuff?" he asked.

Zeke glanced at Charlie. "Just the whole history of this fucked up town, bro. Like the KKK."

Denny wrinkled his face. "The KKK? For cereal?"

I took a drag. "They used to run shit around here. Back in, like, the forties or something," I explained.

"Then the mafia," Charlie said, picking up a pebble and tossing it.

I flicked my cigarette and laughed. "Oh, come on, man. That was just because they locked up some bigwig Don down here and his family moved in." I turned to Denny and took the pipe. "It wasn't a big deal like it sounds. He's just being a shit."

"Holy crap," Denny said, completely ignoring me. "The KKK *and* the mafia? This place is corrupt."

Zeke pulled his knees back up and crossed his arms over them. "And you don't even know the half of it. This place is cursed, bro."

I passed the pipe back to Charlie, and he hit it against his palm. "I told you, guys" he said. "The vortex of weird."

Zeke stretched back on his arms. "Weird as fuck. Like, there's supposed to be a whole network of tunnels underneath town. The KKK used them for their Grand Poobah meetings or some shit. There's even supposed to be one under the high school boiler room."

Denny whacked my arm. "Dude!" Before I could complain or explain, he turned back to Zeke. "We found a tunnel in my basement yesterday!"

Zeke leaned forward. "Say what now?"

I rolled my eyes and rested my head against the wall.

"Yeah, dude. A few bricks came out of the wall yesterday and we found a tunnel back there." Denny hit my arm again. "Didn't we?"

"Yeah. And stop whacking me, man."

He ignored me again. "I wanted to check it out, but this guy," he jabbed a thumb in my direction, "was being a pussy about it."

"I wasn't being a pussy. It's just a dumb idea." I leaned forward and took the pipe back from Charlie.

"Bro, I don't blame him," Zeke said. "This whole fucking town is haunted. Prisons, houses, you name it. Shit, even the Golden Faire down the road," he said, hitching his thumb over his shoulder. "It shut down twenty years ago after this dude went through and shot everyone."

"Holy shit!"

"You been up to the old mines yet?" Charlie asked him.

Denny shook his head, totally enthralled. "Nuh uh."

"Oh, bro." Zeke leaned back on his arms again, stretched his legs out, and looked over at me. "Bro, we should totally take him up there."

"Fucking spooky as hell up there," Charlie said. "I'm not lying, neither."

"You think this all has something to do with the tunnel in my basement?"

Gravel crunched nearby, and we stopped talking to look up at the couple lurking over us.

"Hi," Camille said, as if nothing had happened at all.

Chapter 6

Camille was short and frizzy and Steve was tall and greasy. They had matching anarchy symbols tattooed on the padding between their thumb and forefinger, which they'd given to each other at home with a sewing needle and pen ink. They were running a low rent, teenage prostitution business and from what I'd heard Camille's going rate was twenty for a lay. Or you could pay with a CD, or batteries, or whatever the fuck else you had on hand. I'd grown up with her at the trailer park, had known her since she was the weird, skinny kid allergic to everything with crooked bangs an inch too short. Her boob was the first one I'd ever seen up close and personal and that was only because she wanted to show me that her nipple piercing was getting gangrene. Lucky me.

It was also with Camille that I'd broken my promise to Shane, just that once, and it hadn't even been the real deal. We'd been up in the boonies and she'd taken my thirty bucks and snorted the aspirin with me like it was some kind of good shit, then her and her brother and his fuckhead buddies had stolen my clothes and ditched me up there, butt ass naked.

Hadn't talked to her since.

"Hey," we all said back to her, then I flicked my cigarette down the alley and looked over at Denny. "You wanna get out of here?" I asked.

"Bro, come on. Don't be a dick," Zeke said.

Denny looked between me and the couple, obviously confused, but shrugged anyway. "Sure, I guess," he said.

I pushed myself up and Camille and Steve took a step back to give me room to pass.

"Later," she said, crossing her arms. She was wearing a thermal with thumb holes cut out of the sleeves, I was almost positive it used to be mine.

"Yeah, later," I said to her. "Ready?" I asked Denny.

He lugged himself up, pushing off the gravel asphalt half bent over with his palms on the ground, and then we stepped around everyone and headed towards the road.

"Who was that?" Denny asked.

"Nobody."

"Didn't seem like nobody, dude."

"Just forget about it," I said.

"Well, shit," he said, letting it go. "I was kinda hoping to go with Zeke up to those mines. Think we'll run into him again?"

"Yeah, for sure." We came up to the sidewalk and stopped. "Where to now?" I asked.

"You wanna go check out the Golden Faire?"

"Sure," I shrugged. "Why not?"

The Golden Faire Hotel. The tallest—and oldest—building in town. It sat on the last block of Main Street, right where the road ran up to the gates of Old Max before curving left back into the highway.

We crossed over and made our way down the dark block. It was *always* dark on that side—prison front property isn't a real big seller, you know— and the only two lights came from the end of the road: the orange prison lights and the Golden Faire's blue neon sign, flashing like it was the last stop before hell.

"So what's the deal with this place?" Denny asked.

I took a drag. "There was this one guy. Donald Geist, right? Totally went off his rocker twenty years ago and drove to the motel with a couple of rifles.

So he goes in, shoots the clerk, takes the master key, then makes his way upstairs and starts opening doors and shooting the people inside. Some of 'em came running out, and he just popped them off too, until pretty much everyone was dead. There was so much blood and shit to clean up that they had to close down for a while."

"Holy fuck," Denny said.

"I know, right? Anyways, they open back up and it's a little spooky, you know? Nothing major. But then after they executed Donald Geist, people started saying that they could hear his boots going down the hall every night. So after a while no one really stayed there anymore, and they had to shut down."

"Jesus," Denny breathed.

I puffed the air out of my cheeks. "Yeah."

We passed the mommy crew on their way back towards Comet's—all the pregnant chicks who *said* they couldn't drink or smoke, but who still did their hair and makeup and came downtown to party, anyway—and then it got quiet again, the sound of our footsteps echoing down the hollow street.

Denny and I finally came up to the Golden Faire and peered into the windows. Without fail, even though it'd been closed for decades, the lights in the red velvet lobby were always on and gleaming over a polished brass bar that was always empty.

Denny walked to the door and pushed, both of us expecting it to rattle on a lock. When it opened wide, Denny looked over at me with his mouth and eyes opened wide in big, excited "O"s.

"*Oooh* shit, dude," he said. "Come on, let's check it out."

"Someone's probably in there, man."

"Great, maybe they'll give us a tour." And then he was inside.

Chapter Seven

The story went that the Stewart brothers had built the Golden Faire so the miners would spend their money in town on liquor and poker instead of sending it home back east. And once they built the hotel, the prostitutes came, and soon turned into mothers, and then wives. Then those families had needed a store and a church and a school and that was how Stewartville was born.

It was musty inside the lobby and I itched to run my finger across the fine layer of dust covering the bar.

"Don't touch anything," I reminded Denny, speaking low as I followed him left through the doorway and out of sight of the windows.

A wide staircase led up to the rooms and Denny stopped at the bottom. "Hello?" he called.

Nothing.

"Let's go check it out," he whispered.

I had always been curious about the place, and it was pretty cool inside. The stairs ran up a gold and cream wallpapered hall with golden banisters on either side that we carefully avoided touching. Plush red carpeting padded our footsteps and a few sconces lit the way, turned down low in soft, golden light, so that our life-sized shadows climbed the stairs beside us.

But when we got to the first floor landing and turned the corner the decor took a serious nosedive. The faded wallpaper was peeling, revealing the black and moldy drywall beneath. The stained carpet was half torn up and wires hung exposed from the outlets.

We kept going, stopped at the first open door and looked in.

Pale light filtered through the room's dust-smeared window onto a bare, stained mattress; a dusty vanity; and a wardrobe with its door hanging from the hinge. Shadows sat heavy around them.

The hotel creaked.

Denny nudged me. "Did you hear that?" he whispered.

I nodded.

"Hello?" he called, his voice shakier than it had been before. We turned our backs on the room and that bothered me almost as much as the noise had. It was one thing to face an open hall. It was totally another to turn your back on people possibly climbing out from under the shadows behind you.

But nothing moved in the silence.

"I don't think anyone's here, dude," Denny whispered.

We kept creeping forward, me trailing behind, wishing I wasn't so high, wishing I could light up, until we came to the second room where furniture was stacked up like a pile of petrified flesh. Butchered, curved, scrolling table legs. Tapered, smoothed armrests.

A single, deep piano note cut into the quiet and then clung there.

"Holy shit," Denny whispered in the street lit hallway. The vibrato thinned and faded. "What do we do?"

Fucking Denny. It was his idea to come here.

"I don't know," I said. "Head back down?"

"Are you crazy?"

"I don't know," I hissed again. "I was just thinking—"

A shadow crept up the stairwell, looming along just ahead of its owner, and even through the thick carpeting came the sound of its footsteps.

Thud.

Thud.

Thud.

"Oh my god," Denny whispered as we backed down the hall. "It's that crazy dude's ghost."

The shadow was almost at the landing now and we slapped at each other to get going, tripping over our feet as we scrambled into the last room and carefully, noiselessly, shut the door.

The room was empty. Nowhere to hide.

The footsteps crept down the hall.

Thud.

Thud.

Thud.

A door creaked open.

"The fire escape," I whispered, moving across the room as the footsteps resumed down the hall. A second door open and closed.

We stood on either side of the windowsill—turning orange in the glow of lights from Old Max—and tugged upward, keeping our sides turned to the door so it couldn't sneak up on us. Another door opened down the hall, the window budged, and a small draft of fresh air hit my knuckles as the sirens of Old Max started wailing.

Chapter Eight

"Oh my god, dude," Denny said over the siren. "Do you think that's him?"

"I don't know, man, but it makes more sense than a ghost." I grunted, tugging up on the window. Through it came the sounds of cheering as the kids down at Comet's celebrated the escape with whistles and the smashing of bottles.

"He's gonna kill us, isn't he?" Denny whispered again, helping me push. "Seriously, man?"

"How do you think he got out?"

"I don't know."

"You think through the tunnels?"

"Will you shut up about the fucking tunnels for a minute?" Another grunt and the window cracked open a little more.

He shut up, and I felt like a dick. But it was Denny, so he didn't shut up for long.

"You ever seen one before?" he asked.

"What, an escapee?"

"Yeah."

I couldn't say for sure if I had. It wasn't like a prisoner on the run came right up to you and announced themselves or anything, so you were just left wondering. Wondering if the pale-faced man walking on the other side of the dark street was a man desperate for a certain freedom, or just a man desperate for the normal sort.

"I don't know," I said. Again. Because Denny kept asking stupid questions like I was mayor of the place.

Thud.

Thud.

Thud.

A door opened and closed. Closer now.

We shut up and struggled with the window as the footsteps continued down the hall, then froze when the knob rattled behind us.

"We fucking forgot to lock it," I hissed, more to myself than Denny.

The door opened with a long, slow creak and the old man stared at us, his arms and legs limp, his body swaying like a drunkard. Thin white hair stuck out in every direction from his liver-spotted scalp, and I would have known he was a prisoner by the gray smock and slacks even without the letters DOC stenciled on them.

I guess that answered Denny's question.

"Don't move," I told Denny. But we both turned instinctively and pressed our backs to the window, anyway. The old man swept his eyes over the room.

"Do something," Denny hissed.

"What the fuck am I supposed to do?"

"I don't know. But it's just some ninety-year old dude, dude. I'm pretty sure if something goes wrong, we can take him."

I'd been trying not to look the guy directly in the eyes, but somehow that's right where I wound up, connecting with wet and soupy pupils that connected right back with mine. The old man gave me a crooked yellow grin.

"Hey mister," Denny blurted. "Nice night, huh?"

It was my turn to whack him. "Dude, shut the fuck up!"

But it was too late. The old man took several shuffling steps towards us.

"They're coming," he said.

Denny and I pressed ourselves closer to the window. Lights, blue and red, flashed across the walls as a police siren squawked by.

"Yeah, man," I said. "I think they are."

"They'll come for you, too."

Didn't I know it. You know what sucks? Being a teenager in a town that constantly reminds you that there are serious consequences to your actions. It was never just smoking a bowl or having a few beers with friends in good old-fashioned, All-American fun. Nope. It always felt like you were just taking one step closer to the prisons, one step closer to the inevitable. My gut settled, and I almost opened my mouth, to commiserate or some other dumb shit, when the man opened his wide.

"Run!" he shrieked.

Denny and I both about jumped out of our skin and can you believe that shithead grabbed at my jacket like I was gonna save his life? Who was the pussy again?

"Run, motherfuckers, run!" Spit flew out of the old man's mouth and he grabbed at the fluffs of his hair. He spun in circles, pulling at himself, his clothes, his feet, and then just as suddenly as he had started he stopped. He stared at us, panting, and then he started giggling. Not laughing, *giggling*. Like a creepy ass kid.

Denny grabbed onto me tighter but instead of charging for us the old man turned to the wall and started beating his head into it.

"Holy shit! Dude!" Without thinking I jumped forward and pulled him away, grabbing him by his thin shoulders to hold him back from killing himself. Blood streamed down his face and I swear to God it looked like he had left a tooth behind in the plaster.

Then Denny was grabbing at me and pulling me away.

"Come on, dude!" he said.

We scrambled out the window and down the iron-grate stairs.

We jumped down, dashed down the alley, and then held back at the end and waited as police cars went flying down the street.

"They're coming!" the man screeched again, his voice trailing through the open window.

"Let's get the fuck out of here," Denny said, and with no further discussion we hauled ass around the corner.

"Freeze!"

I looked over my shoulder at the cop down at the opposite end of the street, hoping like hell he didn't have a nervous trigger finger.

"He's in there!" I yelled, pointing back at the Golden Faire. The cop looked up at the hotel and Denny and I disappeared around the corner.

We ran, turning north here and west there, until several blocks stood between us and downtown. Then it was just Denny and I alone on a dark neighborhood street.

We stopped in a space between the streetlights and I knelt down next to a parked car to catch my breath.

Denny bent over and put his hands on his knees "Ho-lee fuck!" he breathed. Then he laughed, and just as quickly rose back up and threw a hand in the air. "Can you believe that shit? We just talked to a fucking escaped lunatic! *And* we ran from the cops."

"Calm down, dude. It's not fucking Disneyland." My heart was racing a mile a minute, and I felt sick to my stomach. Fucking needed to quit smoking.

"He was fucking cuh-ray-zee! Did you see that shit?"

I wiped my forehead with the back of my hand and pulled out a cigarette. I lit it, then rested my head back against the car door, thanking my lucky stars it didn't have an alarm. From down the way we heard a cop squawk his siren a few times.

Denny knelt down next to me. "You think that old guy got away again?"

I took a drag. "Nah, they're probably just clearing the streets. They do that when there's an escape." I flicked my ash onto the dark asphalt. "Night's over. No point going back to Comet's."

I pulled myself up, and we started making our way back to Denny's, ducking and jogging through the intersections to avoid the patrol cars crisscrossing through the streets. Shutting the barn door after the horse got out, I guess.

With a block left to go, an engine sputtered towards us in the night and a second later headlights appeared. The car passed beneath the streetlights: A rusty, yellow Datsun. I stood up straighter and stepped out into the road.

Zeke pulled up and rolled down the window. A cloud of smoke escaped from around him, swirling up into the dark sky above.

"Hey! I was looking for you guys," he said, leaning across the passenger seat. "Did you wanna go check out the mines or what?"

Denny looked at me. "Hell yeah. I'm down," he said.

"You know, Curiosity Killed the Cat," I reminded him.

"Yeah, but satisfaction brought it back," he grinned.

I laughed and shoved him towards the car. "Get in, smart ass."

"You coming?" Zeke asked.

I peered into the window across Denny's seat. "We're just going for a quick drive, right? Cause I need to get home and check on Nana soon."

"Yeah, bro." He winked at Denny. "We'll just smoke a bowl, scare him a little, then leave."

"All right then, man." I hit the roof of the car and moved to the back door. "Let's make this quick."

Chapter Nine

Supposedly, it was our isolated, hardscrabble landscape that made us a perfect spot for all those prisons. See, there was nowhere to run and nowhere to hide, being out in bumfuck Egypt and all. Shit, the nearest town was still a hundred miles down the pockmarked road. But I'd always thought it was something else, too. There was an ugliness and a hopelessness about Stewartville, where misery and waste just seemed to hang in the air above us.

Now, some people might describe that as a heavy feeling, and *we* were heavy, sure. We dragged our feet down sidewalks cracked and choked with weeds, past abandoned storefronts and a market that smelled like old stale blood, and into neighborhoods with nothing but dirt front yards and rusted chain-link fences. But the misery itself? That was like helium, lighter than air, and it quivered above us in the wide open sky so you couldn't even lift your head in prayer without having to face it.

And yet somehow the old mine felt even worse than that.

When we hit the gravel road, Zeke turned off the radio to give Denny the full, creepy effect of the dark silence. Our tires crunched over the rocks and the highlights pushed the dark away from the car, letting us see a few feet of dusty road that seemed to stretch forever into the void. Dried weeds ran alongside us, as brittle and white as bones.

Every once in a while, something out in all that blackness would catch the glare of our lights as we drove and come swimming out of the dark towards us like a freaky, glowing, apparition until we were close enough to recognize it for what it really was: an abandoned fridge or washing machine.

But to be honest, those appliances unsettled me more than any figments of my imagination. They were reminders, too. No matter how happy life seemed, all it amounted to was a wasteland full of rusted junk.

There was a break in the weeds and Zeke turned the car down the side road. We bounced down the ruts and ridges until a stone foundation rose out of the night. We came to a stop in front of it and dust floated over the concrete steps.

Zeke shut off the car and slowly our eyes adjusted to the sliver of light coming from the moon.

"Welcome to the mine, bro," he said, looking over at Denny. "The most cursed spot in Stewartville."

"This is it?" Denny asked. "There's nothing out here."

"Well, the actual mine is over there in that hill," Zeke pointed out the window but in the night Denny could only take his word for it, "but the road doesn't go back that far anymore and it's been blasted closed anyhow. And there's a bunch of old foundations scattered out here from houses and stuff. But this—" he pointed out the windshield at the foundation. "Is the old schoolhouse."

"And it's haunted or what?"

"Oh *yeah*, man" He shifted in his seat to sit against the window and look at Denny. "OK, listen, right? The Stewartville Massacre. The miners up here went on a strike or something and it turned into this big war between the mining company and the workers. Men dead all over the streets, the mines blasted closed."

"It's how we got Old Max," I said, lighting a cigarette.

Denny turned and looked back at me. "Whaddya mean?"

"Because," Zeke said, lifting his ass to pull a pack of smokes from his pocket. "The mining company arrested all the surviving men, but they didn't have a jail big enough to hold them. So they kept 'em locked up in the Golden Faire at night and had 'em build Old Max during the day."

He pulled a joint out of the pack and handed it to Denny. The dark rushed up against the car as he lit the lighter, leaving us in the small pocket of light within. The flame went out. The paper crackled into embers, and the darkness relaxed and thinned out around us once more.

Denny wheezed smoke out. "All these people died or went to prison just because they went on strike?" he asked. "That's kinda fucked up, man."

"Story of Stewartville," Zeke took the joint back. "The schoolteacher? Her husband was one of the men buried alive in the mines. So she got her revenge by setting the school on fire." He took a hit. "With all the students in it."

"Damn," Denny breathed. A gust of wind blew against the car, whistling against the windows, and the weeds at the foot of the schoolhouse steps bent and bobbed their stalks casting thin shadows in the moonlight.

"Legend has it that if you park here overnight and lock the doors, you'll wake up with handprints all over your car. If you forget to lock the doors..." Zeke took a hit, snorted back a cough. "Well, if you forget to lock up and they get in, then you pretty much wake up dead."

"No shit? Have you tried it?"

Zeke shook his head and offered me the joint. I passed. I got the weed demons enough at home, fuck getting them out here.

"Let's get out and go check it out" Denny said.

"Yeah, all right," Zeke said. He swiveled in his seat and turned on the lights so we could see.

We opened the car doors and stepped out into air that was cooler but not necessarily fresher. There was always a thickness to it out here that seemed to seep into my lungs and rot away at my soul.

I pulled my jacket closed as we moved around to the front of the car and went up the steps. There'd been graffiti along the inside of the foundation for as long as I'd been going up there; pentagrams, cuss words, penises— you know, normal stuff. But tonight I saw something else. Two words recently spray painted in tall, black letters covered one side of the wall.

They're Coming

Chapter Ten

"Dude!" Denny whacked my arm. "Holy shit! That's what that prisoner said!"

I rubbed my bicep and side-eyed him. "*Yeah*. I was there."

"What prisoner?" Zeke asked.

"That guy who escaped Old Max tonight? We ran into him downtown—in the Golden Faire, actually! —and he was freaking out and saying 'they're coming' and then he started bashing his head against the wall. Oh! And we heard the piano."

Zeke looked over at me and frowned. "Yo, that's some crazy ass shit, bro. For real."

"He just meant the cops were coming," I said, taking a drag.

"Then what's this shit?" Denny asked, pointing at the foundation. Our shadows stood across from us, staring back.

"I don't know, man. It's probably just a coincidence. You really think some ninety-year-old con came up here with a can of spray paint? Get real."

"Dude, why do you gotta be such a downer?" Denny asked. "Just have fun with it, damn." He turned to Zeke. "You shoulda seen him when we found that tunnel. Scared as hell, man."

I rolled my eyes. "For the last time, I *wasn't* scared. I'm just not a fucking idiot." I took a drag. "That thing could cave in, you know."

Apparently, there was something funny about that, because Denny and Zeke got the pot giggles. I flicked my cigarette out into the dirt and hopped down from the steps. "Fuck y'all," I said. "Let's just get outta here."

Their laughter followed me all the way back to the car, and they were *still* giving me hell by the time we headed down the rutted road. But finally they got quiet and Zeke flipped on the radio.

I laid my head back against the seat right as the blue light flooded the back window. The three of us turned our heads and squinted at the high beams behind us.

"Yo, what the fuck?" Zeke said. "Where the hell did they come from?"

My scalp tingled.

"Dude, get the fuck out of here," Denny said.

"I can't go any faster through these ruts, bro."

"It's probably just some stoners giving us hell," I said, lighting another smoke. Wouldn't be the first time someone got pranked up there. "Or it's fucking tweakers." That was the worst-case scenario, especially if they were out here tripping balls and thinking we were undercover FBI or some shit.

We got to the turn and Zeke gassed it; the dust kicking up around us and the gravel shredding beneath the tires, and the car fishtailed out onto the main road. His hands wrestled the wheel—back and forth, this way and that—and once he got it straightened out, he floored it again. Denny and I twisted around in our seats and watched out the rearview window for the guy to follow, but the car idled back at the turn, the make and model invisible in the glare of its lights.

We flew down the road and the lights got smaller and then went out altogether. "I think they're done fucking with us," I said, turning around.

"Holy shit!" Zeke yelled. He slammed on the brakes and the front wheel drive swung the back tires around behind us. I held onto Denny's seat until we had come to a horizontal stop in the middle of the road.

"What the fuck was that?" I asked, my heart racing. We'd almost fucking ate it in a ditch.

Zeke kept his hands on the wheel and looked around. "You guys didn't fucking see that?"

"See what?" Denny asked.

"There was someone in the fucking road." Zeke opened the car door and stood just inside of it, looking over the car at the side of the road.

Denny turned in his seat and looked out the window. "What the fuck…" he breathed, his head bobbing up and down as he searched the darkness.

I looked out at the weeds and into the thick blanket of night. "I don't see anything, man."

Zeke got back in the car and put it in gear. "I swear to god to you, I saw something."

"You smoke too much," I said. "Nothing's out there."

As soon as the words were out of my mouth headlights blinded us once again, flooding the car in bright white light. The three of us raised our hands to our eyes and started shouting.

They'd been driving dark.

"Fucking go!" Denny and I yelled. *"Go! Go!"*

"Fuuuuck!" Zeke threw the car in reverse, backed half the car off the road, then floored it again, the rear end sliding this way and that as it gained traction. We flew over the bumps, skid around the curves, and the lights stayed right behind us. My heartbeat was pumping, and I smoked the shit out of my cigarette, not sure if I was going to die because some meth heads were gonna get me or because the car was gonna fly off the road and flip. And then we hit the paved part of the road, bounced over the rain dip and scratched his bumper, and flew down the street into town.

"They're not behind us anymore," I said, watching out the rear window. "They never left the dirt road."

Zeke glanced back in the rearview mirror. "You sure?"

"Yeah, I would've seen 'em in the streetlights." I turned back and around and tossed my cigarette out the window.

"Fucking A'," Denny said as Zeke slowed the car down inside the neighborhood. "That was fucking insane."

"Yeah, no shit," I said.

There was a pause and the three of us looked at each other. Then we busted up laughing, adrenaline coursing through our veins and making us high.

Chapter Eleven

We pulled up to Denny's house, dark between the two brick buildings, and he and I both climbed out while Zeke idled the car.

"Hey, I'll catch you guys later," Denny said, giving me a handshake and a fist bump.

"See ya." I took his spot in the passenger side and lit another smoke as he headed up the walk. Zeke chewed his lip and watched as Denny made it inside.

"Something weird about that house, bro," he said. He put the car in gear and pulled away.

"You mean like a tunnel?" I took a drag and dropped my hand out the window.

We drove through the empty streets, crossed the quiet highway, and entered the south side of town.

"Hey, so my mom's getting out next week," he said. The dark salvage yard flew past us, the bodies of cars black and twisted carcasses that had fallen in defeat before the building.

"Nice, man. Congrats."

"Yeah, I'm super stoked, bro." He pulled up across the road from the trailer park and idled the car for a minute. "After graduation we're out of here. Gonna head up to Iowa and live with my grandparents. Get out of this hellhole." He picked up the baggie in the console, dropped it back in. "Gotta quit this stuff. Don't wanna mess it up."

"Yeah. That's awesome, dude. And you'll be fine, don't worry about it."

"Thanks. So, anyway, she wanted me to make sure I told you that your mom misses you and she's being moved and could use a friendly face and stuff."

I rubbed my cheek and opened the door. Zeke's mom had been transferred to my mom's unit two years ago, and they acted like it was the PTA up in there now. "Yeah, all right."

"When's the last time you went?"

I flicked my cigarette out the door. "I don't know, man. Back when she got her new prison teeth."

"You know I'm just asking 'cause I gotta hear about it." He glanced over at me, being all shrinky and shit.

"Right. Yeah, I know." I stepped out and braced myself on the car, looking in. "Thanks for the ride, man. Talk to you later."

He gave me a fist bump and then I shut the door and made my way around the back of the car, stopping about halfway down the bumper.

Zeke stuck his head out the window. "You forget something?"

I looked up from the muddy handprints on the trunk but kept my mouth shut. "Nah, sorry, man," I said. "Go get your car washed."

He waved, pulled out, and I crossed the empty road into the lot. Tin boxes aren't very soundproof and the trailer park hummed with the sound of life: TVs, radio's, parties, some dude and his old lady bitching at each other. And Shep was out in his pool, like always.

He was a sixty-year-old player and had taken a kiddie pool and built a deck around it. And I'm not talking about those three feet above ground pools either. This thing was four feet across and six inches deep. Almost every night he'd sit out in his "spa" with his beer on the deck and entertain some of the older ladies in the park. Some of his friends would come by and you'd think they were somewhere great with the Christmas lights up and the drinks flowing and Marvin Gaye playing on the little radio. It was the most ridiculous shit I'd ever seen, but hey, they were happy. And Shep was always good for a cigarette or two, even if they were menthol.

But with all that going on, you didn't even need cable here. All you had to do was sit on your porch and watch the drama unfold.

And that's exactly what Camille was doing. Her family owned the park and lived in the property manager's house in the middle of the lot. It was an old wooden place that had turned grey with time and she was sitting out on the sagging steps next to a broken down portable dishwasher.

I was just gonna ignore her, like I did every other night, but it was obvious she'd been crying. I sighed and stuck my hands in my pockets.

From the light of the bug zapper and the single crooked light pole above their place, I could tell she'd gotten rid of the pale foundation, the heavy eyeliner and mascara, the black lipstick. Sitting there in a baggy sweater with her freckles shining through, she looked like the girl I'd grown up with. The one who used to listen to Vanilla Ice on her Barbie radio and practice dance moves in the dirt yard with her shirt tied up into a halter.

Six months ago her favorite brother, Roy, had been in a shootout with and got killed by the cops. He'd been one of Stewartville's main meth dealers and for a while business had been good. See, it wasn't just all that funding that made prisons so profitable, and he'd had plenty of customers both inside and out. But that shit never lasts, and he didn't go down easy. Or sober. There'd been a lawsuit, but it hadn't gone well.

"You okay?" I called.

She sniffled and nodded but didn't make any move to get up or call me over. I pinched the cherry from my smoke, stuck the half behind my ear, then went inside and checked on Nana. She was sleeping, so I shut the door quietly and went back down the hall to the kitchen where I found another letter waiting for me in the glow of the stove's light. I slid it into my back pocket and then grabbed a spoon and shoveled up the canned chili Shane had left out on the stove.

Camille was still outside when I went back to the porch to smoke, and I could feel her eyes on me as I sat down on the steps and lit up. I kept my head down, looked at the stairs, took another drag and pulled out the letter while Mr. and Mrs. Mullet started screaming at each other three trailers down.

I could pretty much imagine everything written inside; I'd gotten enough of these things throughout the years. Apologies, promises that she was better now, promises about what we'd do after. Then anger, blame, and ranting after she'd scored a line and had another setback.

The door to the big house clapped shut, and I took a drag and looked over. The light in Camille's room came on, shining against the pink sheet she used as a curtain, and as I watched her moving around behind it, I wondered if she'd ever realized I could see her changing back there.

I chuckled and looked away. Of course she did. I remembered the first year we realized we weren't kids anymore. Man, were we rolling in spare change and smokes. All she had to do was bat her eyes and the old VFW men would literally give her the flannels off their backs. I had one tied around my waist, in fact.

But then the clothes had gotten baggy, and the hustling had stopped. No more free passes. It was an eye for an eye. And then once she'd hooked up with Steve it became a whole new ballgame. Life was ugly like that.

I exhaled, the smoke drifted away into the night, and Camille's bedroom light went out. And then it got quiet. Couldn't even hear the crickets. I shoved the letter back in my pocket and started thinking about those muddy handprints on Zeke's car. It hadn't even been wet out there, so I didn't know how they'd managed that. And there was something else, too.

The handprints had been small. Like a kid's hands.

The energy outside changed, like there was some weird imperceptible shift in the air, and I thought about how alone I was out there, but also how I didn't *feel* alone either. I took a drag and tried to avoid looking at the shadows, shadows that were growing out from beneath cars and trailers like outstretched arms, but not looking at them made it worse. Like the more I avoided looking, the more something really was there.

"Fuck this," I said, letting the sound of my voice scare away the monsters like I had when I was five. I flicked my cigarette out into the dirt, pushed myself up and then went inside, trying not to run like I was being chased. I turned off the lights, put up the chain, and headed to bed in the orange glow of the lights.

I looked up at my window as the sirens started to wail, feeling like whatever had been out front a minute ago was now standing right on the other side of the glass, just waiting and watching me.

Chapter Twelve

The next afternoon I was lounging in the recliner and eating Cheetos in my boxers when the phone rang. I picked it up first ring so as not to wake Shane sleeping on the couch, even though he was soundly snoring through the gunshots and explosions coming from the TV.

"Dude." Denny said.

"What's up, man?"

"You gotta get over here."

"I'm busy."

"No, seriously. You *have* to get over here. *Now*." I heard his mom in the background and Denny lowered his voice. "Come on, man."

I sighed and picked up my pack. One smoke left.

"All right, fine," I said. The phone went dead in my hand.

I grunted and pulled myself up with a heavy sigh. Not that it was difficult work. I was skinny as shit. I padded quietly through the living room, my boxers barely hanging on to my hip bones, and then crawled through my bedroom door, across the mattress, and then hung over the side to dig around for some clothes in the closet. Through the wall I could hear Nana's soaps goin' and I knew she'd be good for the next few hours.

I hopped down the deck stairs and started walking that back road, the prisons off to my left, barbed wire glinting beneath the sun like mirages of light.

I had nightmares about them as a kid. There was this book I read when I was four, *Harold and the Purple Crayon*, and as I laid in bed and looked at the pictures of him drawing his world, my heart would start beating with every straight line that became a box. Then I'd drift away to sleep, sure in my dreams that Harold would fall from the moon straight down into those prisons.

Because they just sat there waiting for you, as sure as heaven and hell did.

I took a right, prisons at my back, went down the hill past the burger stand, and got my smokes. No Marlboro's for me. No sir. Good old GPC: Generic Pack Cigarettes.

At Denny's, I scuffed my cigarette out on the curb, went up the walk with a heavy sigh, and knocked on the door.

"What's going on?" I asked, as he led me to the basement.

"My mom just left," he said as we headed down the stairs. We got to the bottom, and he grabbed a flashlight off the coffee table. "Here, take this."

"What? Why?" But just as I asked, I noticed he had pulled the bricks back out of the wall again. My heart sank.

"So we can check out the tunnel, dude." He walked over to the hole and squatted down.

"Man, come on. I'm not going in there."

"Oh, come *on*, dude." He rested his elbows on his knees and looked at me. "Stop being such a pussy. Aren't you the least bit curious?"

The hole was gaping now, grinning even. As Denny waited for my answer, he switched on the light and shone it in. I looked in at that dirt floor and rounded walls and knew sure as shit that I wasn't the least bit fucking curious.

"Fine. Fuck." Denny narrowed his eyes at me, having read the refusal on my face. "Can you just keep an eye out at least?"

"You're seriously going in? What about the mold?"

"Fuck yeah I'm going in, dude." And as I watched, silent, he set the flashlight down inside the hole, got down on his knees, and began squeezing himself in. As he scooted through, his grey shirt rode up over his chest and the bricks scratched red marks along his gut. And then, slowly, it was just his ass was hanging out, the top bricks catching the edge of his jeans and showing me his crack and the tiny red bumps there. That's all I saw, Denny's bent legs and ass sticking out of the wall. It was almost hilarious, if not for the fact that all I could think of was a snake eating a rat.

"Fuck."

I could barely hear him. "What's wrong?"

"I'm stuck."

Images flashed through my mind. Denny, stuck in the wall for eternity. The wall collapsing and crushing him. Me, having to put my hands on his soft, fatty ass to push him through.

I watched him wiggle and squirm. "Dude, fucking help me out," he said.

I spoke down to his legs. "In or out?"

"Push me *in*."

Keeping my hands in my pockets, I put my foot on his ass and pushed against it.

"You motherfucker," he said. "Are you seriously fucking using your foot?"

I laughed then. "I'm not fucking grabbing your ass, dude. It looks like you don't even wash that shit." I pushed harder. The bricks scratched his tailbone and then his ass was over the wall as he was scrambling in.

"Damn, dude!" he said, his voice echoing inside the tunnel. "This shit is crazy."

I knelt down and peered in.

Denny waved the flashlight around and all I could make out was the packed dirt walls and dirt floor running off into a circle of darkness. Then he took a few more steps in.

"Where are you going?"

"I'm gonna check it out."

"Man, we don't even know if this is safe."

"It's fine. I'll just go a little ways up."

I watched him retreat down the tunnel, swinging the flashlight left and right, his head swiveling around on his neck.

"You hear that?" he called back.

"No. What?"

"Like a scratching noise."

"It's probably just a rat or something."

"I'm gonna go see."

"A rat? Come on, man, just get out. Let's go smoke a bowl or something."

But he ignored me and started walking forward again. "Hey! There's a turn up here," he said.

"Hey, man—"

But it was too late. I watched his light disappear behind a wall of darkness.

"Hey!" he called a second later, his voice thin and distant. "It's been boarded up and I think something's stuck behind it. Come help me. "

"Fuck that. Let's just go, dude." My heart was pounding a little harder now and I felt tense all over. I was fucking uncomfortable, and hearing this shit secondhand wasn't helping either.

"Fine," he called. "Just hold on." And then it went quiet again.

I waited, staring into the black, until I *realized* I was staring into the black. And I got that creepy feeling you get when you think something might be watching you. And the more uncomfortable I felt, the more I could imagine it creeping on me.

I sat back on my heels and dangled my wrist over my knee. Fucking Denny. I wanted a smoke but no way in hell was I leaving him down there.

The front door slammed.

"Denny!"

All I could think was *holy fuck* over and over. My heart started racing, I bent forward and stuck my head in the tunnel.

"Denny! Denny?" Nothing. Not surprising since I had to whisper-shout. "Shit. Denny! Your mom's coming, man."

Footsteps crossed the floor above me.

I jumped up and looked around. My eyes landed on the entertainment center and a second later I had it pushed up against the hole just as the basement door opened.

Denny's mom stared down at me. I waved up to her like a dumbass, probably looking guilty as fuck. Behind me, I heard movement against the back of the entertainment center.

"Hi, Ms. Duncan," I said. Too loudly.

"Where's Denny?"

"Uh, he said he needed to use the bathroom real quick."

She stared at me for a minute and I felt a bead of sweat run through my hairline, itchy as hell.

"I guess I'll look upstairs then."

"Yes, ma'am." I tried not to move but I couldn't help myself. I scratched my head, where the sweat was tickling through my hair.

She cocked her head at me and I quickly dropped my hand.

"I love my son very much," she said.

I didn't know what to say, so I kept my mouth shut.

"That means I want what's best for him. Good grades, a good future." She raised an eyebrow at me. "Good friends. You understand me?"

"Yes, ma'am."

"I could make your life very miserable if you hurt my son. In any way."

Our eyes stayed locked for a minute and then she smiled.

"Well. I'll go look for Denny now."

I didn't move a muscle until she slowly closed the door between us and even then I waited, listening for departing footsteps. That bead of sweat rolled past my eyebrow and down my cheek.

I bet she was the prison block's favorite guard.

It felt like an eternity before I heard her move away from the door. First it was a single creak above me, and then another. And then when I could tell she was walking away I scrambled to the wall and yanked the entertainment stand back. The hole was pitch black, and I dropped down into a squat to look inside.

"Denny!" I hissed. "Denny!"

A light came on. Denny was sitting against the wall, right inside the hole, holding the flashlight up against his chest, his eyes hollow and empty.

"You okay, man?"

He turned his eyes towards me but it was like nothing was there. He wasn't seeing me.

I reached out a hand and shook his shoulder. "Hey!"

The eyes blinked and Denny was back.

"Is she gone?" he asked.

I sat back on my heels. "Yeah."

He scrambled up, the soles of his shoes scratching against the dirt. "Hurry up and help me out of here," he said.

I grabbed his arms and helped to pull him through. He pushed himself out, not even caring about the scratches, and then spun around and started grabbing the bricks out of the tunnel.

"Hurry!" he squeaked. "Help me get the bricks back in."

I dropped to my knees next to him and started stacking the bricks back in place. He was just slamming them down, fumbling quickly to get the next in place, and a few times I almost lost a finger. Then the last one was in, sliding into the hole with a satisfying finality.

Denny got up and stood at one corner of the entertainment stand. "Come on, *help*," he said, barely looking at me. So I went around to the other side and we pushed it back up against the wall, and that's when he finally he put his palms on his knees and took a breath.

"Seriously, man, are you okay?" I asked. "Look, I don't think your mom noticed the—"

"There's something back there," he panted, staying bent over.

"What?"

"I moved the board, right? And then this thing--"

"Denny!"

Our eyes shot up. Footsteps. Fast, stomping footsteps. Denny straightened and turned pale as the reverberations shook the whole house.

Clink.

The bricks tumbled back into the tunnel.

Chapter Thirteen

The basement door flew open and Denny's mom looked down at us, her face red with hate and rage. My heart started pounding, and I told myself it was normal enough. That moms are pissy and on the rag all the time.

"You little asshole," she hissed down at Denny. "You fat, fucking, good-for-nothing, piece of shit."

But sometimes they're not. Sometimes they're just bad.

"You need to leave," she said to me.

I shot my eyes to Denny, looking for some clue as to what the fuck had just happened. "Hey man. You gonna be okay?" I asked.

"*Now!*" she shouted.

I ignored her. "You want me to call someone?"

Denny wouldn't look at me, but he shook his head. "Just go," he mumbled. "Don't worry about it."

There was nothing more I could do. I stood up and ducked my head to avoid eye contact with his mom and went up the stairs. I dreaded every step that brought me closer to her and it made my body burn hot, my skin itchy.

She blocked the doorway until I was a breath away and then moved aside to let me pass. Intimidation tactics, Ms. Duncan? What a gem. But she wasn't my first bully, so I ignored it and turned back around to say bye to Denny. And just as I did, I swear I caught the shadow of something moving behind the entertainment center. I didn't know what it was, if it was just the stress or a trick of the light or what, but that was it for me. I was out.

I hustled by his mom and out of the house. The sun had set, and I hadn't realized we'd been down there so long. Maybe thirty minutes at most.

The black hole.

I pictured myself staring into that tunnel as the hours ticked by, pictured myself not even realizing it, not moving, and it freaked me the hell out.

I turned back at the corner and looked at the little gloomy clapboard house squatted on the lawn. That bad feeling I had before, which had never really left, was back stronger than ever.

When I got home, I tripped on the third step and caught myself on the rail before falling. That's how I noticed that someone had pulled a skirting panel off the crawlspace and threw it into the overgrown weeds next to my old bike.

"Shane?"

A shadow moved across the opening and then he popped his head out. "Hey, little dude," he said. "Grab me a flashlight, will ya?"

I brushed my hands off on my knees. "Man, quit calling me that. I'm not a little kid anymore." But it didn't really bother me anymore. It was better than being called a fat fuck.

He grinned up at me, flashing those slightly yellowed teeth. "Just grab it, will you?"

With some obligatory bitching, I went inside to the kitchen and opened the cupboard beneath the sink. I grabbed his flashlight and on the way back out noticed he'd made Hamburger Helper for dinner. Stroganoff, too, which was the worst fucking one.

I went back out, leaned over the deck rail, and tossed down the flashlight. He missed and reached a hand out to grab it.

"Whaddya need it for, anyway?" I asked.

"I think there's a cat back here somewhere," he said. And then he pulled himself back under and disappeared.

The stairs creaked as I hopped down them. I stepped through the weeds and loose pebbles over to where the hole was and squatted down to look into the crawlspace. Shane was laying prone in the dirt, shining the light over all the random shit that had been shoved back there. I followed the light as it ran over broken coffee pots, boxes of two-liter jugs, and my old car seat.

"You hear that?" he asked. "Like scratching?"

"I don't see any—"

The light hit on a dog kennel, but not the shadows inside of it. A shiver went up my spine and made me think of Denny.

I backed up and sat back on my heels. "Shane."

His voice echoed in the crawlspace. "What's up, little dude?"

I didn't exactly know. All I knew was that bad feeling had come back, making my intestines turn to jelly.

"Just be careful, man." I said.

"Aww, you love me." There was a pause and a grunt as he pulled on something. "Go on inside and eat dinner before it gets cold."

I put a hand on the ground and pushed myself up, getting a fucking goat's head sticker in my thumb, in the process. I picked it out as I walked back to the steps, and when I lifted my head, I locked eyes with Camille.

She was sitting on her porch, smoking and watching our every move with this look she sometimes had. Like Earth was her own private world and the rest of us were just visiting aliens that she found mildly amusing.

I went inside, made a plate of dinner, and fell asleep.

Meanwhile, Denny was across town bashing his mom's skull in with a brick.

WALLS

Chapter Fourteen

Inmates had built most of the buildings in Stewartville and I imagine they cemented every brick laid in place with dark and hateful thoughts.

Just like the one that had bashed in Mrs. Duncan's skull.

I sat in the AV room, tapped my lighter on the table, and chewed my lip. Something weird was going on.

Fucked up shit happened all the time in Stewartville. Throw a rock and I guarantee you would hit someone with a messed up story. Like my mom's uncle. When he was a baby, his parents had abandoned him and his siblings in a shack. The other kids had been a little older than him so they'd stuck him in the oven to keep him warm. With the gas on.

Or shit, just walk into any house in town and you could feel the waiting. Like time paused, angrily waiting for it to catch back up.

But there was an order to things. Misery in Stewartville was a gradual process. It sprouted, blossomed and withered with the seasons. Misery here didn't spread fast and fester like an infection, as it had with Denny.

It killed us slowly.

I thought about that fact, as I stared at the wall, and listened to the new guy finish his recording.

Let me just say that I'd never been that popular in school, probably because I spent too much of my time ditching class to go smoke rather than staying in and making friends. But after Denny killed his mom, I gained a bit of notoriety. Lucky me, right?

Gavin, the kid sitting across from me, seemed to think I had some street cred now. He was one of those jock fucks who had all the teachers fooled, but was really a douchebag with a shitty sense of boundaries. He'd asked me a million questions about Denny. What he was like, did I have any clue, and the number one question: did I help? I could tell him if I did. No judgement.

I *had* made the mistake of telling him about the skits. It was after his fifth or sixth book that he tried one out for himself. To make me laugh, he said, loosen me up a bit. It was a nice thought, but the guy was still a first-class creep.

"Greetings, prisoners of Stewartville, this is your asshole speaking, coming at you live with a public service announcement." From the corner of my eye I could see Gavin look up at me, like I would give him a thumbs up or something. But I just kept spinning my lighter and ignored him. Which is probably what annoyed the shit out of him and made him ramp it up. Guys like him always needed attention, no matter how they got it. And especially Gavin, what with his sister being a star swimmer and all. It wasn't any great secret that she was the golden child, and that their parents went to every one of her meets and none of Gavin's matches.

"Look, stop dropping the soap you dumbass motherfuckers," he continued, his voice losing that joking lilt in favor of a bitter edge. "I can't handle anymore of Big Daddy's cock this month.

"Now, I know what you're thinking. 'But Mr. Asshole, don't you like the way the cum lubes you up for those constipated prison food shits?' And to that I say, 'No! Nyet! Nada!' Have some pride, men. You want to finger—"

"Dude. What are you doing?"

Gavin looked up at me and grinned. I wanted to punch him in his fucking pepperoni face. But I could hear the nervousness cutting across the bottom, too. See, Gavin wasn't as hardcore as he liked people to believe. I'd known him since fourth grade, back when he whispered to me he liked to hold in his shits for as long as possible before running to the can. I knew his mom worked as a nurse over at the hospital and that his dad was a lawyer. They lived over on the nice side of town, in those big, empty homes up on the hillside. And I knew that up until ninth grade he'd been a quiet, nerdy kid. He was playing a part, just like everyone else, right down to his black trench coat.

"What?" he laughed. "It's funny."

"Not really, man," I answered. "It's kinda fucking disturbing."

He leaned back in his seat, crossed his arms and kept giving me that shit-eating grin. "I think they'll like it."

"Yeah. If some fucking cannibal serial killer gets it."

"Exactly."

I scoffed. "You gotta be pretty sick to want to impress fuckers like that, dude."

His face turned red, and he leaned forward towards me. "Not as sick as someone who kills their own fucking mom." The silver pentagram necklace he wore caught the glare of the light and for a second I wanted to twist it around his damn neck.

I stopped spinning the lighter, leaned forward, and set my elbows on the table. "His mom was abusing him, asshole."

"Pfft. Please. That cornfed motherfucker?" He sat back and smirked. "Nah, man. You don't just go and kill your mom. Something's gotta be wrong with you."

"Yo, fuck you." I pushed back out of my chair and grabbed my bag. Partly because he was a prick, partly because I knew he was right. "Finish this fucking shit yourself."

"My family sucks too, but it ain't like I'm gonna go murder them," he called after me. "We all got problems, yo!"

It wasn't until I was outside on the steps digging through my pockets when I realized I'd left my smokes inside. Last thing I wanted to do was see that fuckhead again, but I also didn't want to wait until I found someone to bum smokes or change off of either.

So I went back inside, down the empty hall and around the orange cones where the floor was sagging, back through the dark and dim auditorium, and pulled open the AV door.

Gavin was walking along the room. I watched him, kinda stunned in place for a minute — as he trailed his fingers along the wall and mumbled to himself. It was some creepy looking shit. My heart started pounding, and the room turned hot.

"What the fuck are you doing, man?" I asked.

He jumped and spun around to look at me. "You don't hear that scratching?"

That was three times now. My mouth went dry. I had to swallow before answering. "Nah, I don't hear shit." I swallowed again, my throat like swollen sandpaper, and picked up the cigarettes from the table. "Hey, why don't you just grab your bag and let's go? Ms. Alvarez won't care."

"You seriously don't hear that? It sounds like something is stuck behind the wall." He followed the noise until the shelves blocked his progress and then he squatted down and tried to peer behind them. "Maybe if I can just get one of these bricks loose…"

My mind was fucking racing a mile a minute now and not to sound like a pussy or anything, but I almost wanted to cry. See, I was thinking maybe something *had* crawled out of Denny's basement that night, something terrible, and if so, I was sure it was coming for prick head Gavin, too. I dropped my bag, grabbed his coat, and pulled him away from the wall.

"What the fuck, man?" he asked, stumbling upwards.

It took me a second to think of something to say. "You wanna talk shit about Denny?" I said. "Let's go."

"What, you wanna *fight* me now?"

"Yeah." I shoved him back against the wall. "Come on, man."

He pushed my hands off of him and moved away, eyeing me. "Dude, you're just as nuts as your fucking friend," he said. He bent down, grabbed his bag and, when he came back up, his face had turned a bright and angry red. "Get it the fuck together, man. I'm outta here."

He banged out the door, pissed as hell. I picked up my bag, turned off the light, and looked back over my shoulder at the dark and quiet room.

The darkness stared back.

"Fuck you," I whispered.

I headed downtown and hung out at Comet's for a bit until I met some dude named Travis, who was just passing through town. Comet's was usually pretty fucking dead during the day with only one pool table occupied by serious players, so I went with him to his room to smoke a bowl. And wouldn't you know, there were Camille and Steve, talking to the school's guidance counselor in the side parking lot. As I walked across the asphalt, I watched as she ran a finger down his arm and gave him a look. A look she used to give me when she wanted to share my Popsicle, and that she had since perfected into asking for so much more.

I went in the guy's room and sat down at the shitty, little round table by the window, glancing out the curtains.

"This place is a trip, man," he said, bending under the sink at the back wall. He dug through a bag and came up with his shit. "You know you gotta fucking prison right in the middle of Main?"

"Yeah," I said as Camille headed inside with Mr. Anders. I let the curtain fall back. "They built the town up around it."

He sat down across from me and started picking out seeds. "Sirens went off last night and I almost shit my pants. For real, man."

I laughed at that. "Nah man, don't worry about it. Usually it's just the minimum security guys walking away from work detail." He didn't seem to understand. "Non-violent offenders," I explained with a wave of my hand.

"Well shit, that's not too bad."

I leaned forward. "But this room? Some dude went nuts and killed two of his buddies in here."

His hands froze over the herb. "Holy shit, for real?" he asked, sounding and looking just like Denny. I leaned back and looked away.

"Nah," I said, letting out a deep breath. "I'm just pulling your leg."

Later, when the dude and I brought the chairs outside to get some fresh air, Camille and the sun were both gone. But Steve was still there, sitting in his truck smoking, and once again I wanted to ask him how the fuck he was okay with what she was doing. For all he knew, some guy could wind up choking her with the shower curtain just for kicks.

But after a minute she came out, counting her cash. Some different guy, not the counselor, leaned against the open door frame and smoked a cigarette, watching her walk away with a smug ass look on his face that made me want to punch him.

She caught my eye, stuck her tongue in her cheek, and mimed giving head.

I rolled my eyes and leaned back, crossing my arms over my chest.

"You know that chick?" Travis asked.

"Nah," I lied.

"Man, she was down here last night too." He cracked open a beer. "But I ain't interested in what she's selling, you know?"

"Yeah. No kidding."

I watched as Camille and Steve pulled out of the parking lot and went straight into the burger joint.

"Well, that's it for me, man," I said.

"You heading out?"

"Yeah, man." I stood up and bumped his fist. "Take it easy and good luck on your trip."

I lit a smoke, then jogged across the highway and headed for the tracks. The houses on this side of town were more rundown and empty than over on Denny's side, especially the small shingled ones with their little lean-to kitchens that faced the railroad. They were old starter homes back in the fifties, built for the type of men who were named Arthur and had just started work at the butcher shop after marrying his high school sweetheart Mabel, who stayed home with an apron on and practiced folding napkins like her mother had taught her.

A siren cut through my weed-induced daydreams and I realized I'd made it to the tracks. Glancing down through the smoky yellow light that hovered over the rails, I saw a man walking along just far enough down that I could still make out his shape. I took a drag and watched him, wondering if he was the inmate, looking to hop a train out of town, and then he must have sensed me or something, because he dipped into the weeds and disappeared.

Denny would have wanted to chase him down like we were the Hardy Boys.

I chuckled at that as I crossed the tracks and then kept to myself on the dark and quiet street. Not long after a bobcat started screeching, sounding just like a woman screaming bloody murder. The cries scratched across the dark sky, like nails in black flesh, and I pictured Mabel again, alone in one of those low-ceilinged kitchen add-ons, wailing for Arthur because the man in the weeds had come in through the backdoor and had picked up her rolling pin.

I tried to shut my mind up by reminding myself it was just a bobcat. Though in Stewartville, I guess you were never sure until you read the news.

Either way, the screams and the siren followed me all the way home. When I got there, Shane was still under the crawlspace just like he'd been last night and again early this morning.

"Hey, you okay under there?" I called, standing at the bottom of the steps.

"Yeah," his muffled voice called back. "I keep hearing the damn thing, I just can't catch it."

"Man, who cares? It's just a cat."

"There're all kinds of shit it can get into down here," he said.

"Yeah, exactly. *Shit,*" I mumbled. But I left it alone, went in for food and wound up staring at an empty stove. I turned around and stepped right back out.

"Hey!" I called, leaning over the railing of the deck. "What's for dinner?"

His head popped out. "Sorry, little dude, I've been busy. You'll have to find something."

I turned back to the door but paused as a beat-up old Cadillac pulled into the lot and slowed to a stop at our place. The side window went down and a man and woman, both skin and bones, both licking their lips and scratching their faces, peered out at me.

"Hey," the guy whisper-called, leaning over Elvira, Mistress of Meth. "Did you order the muffins?"

"Um. *No.*"

"Look, don't give me any shit you little prick."

The woman glared at me like *I* was the piece of shit.

"Man, get your crusty ass out of here." I said back. "No one ordered any of your damn muffins."

There was rattling from under the trailer as Shane pulled himself out from the skirting.

"Go inside, little dude." He told me as he walked towards the car, wiping his hands free of dirt. "I gotta talk to my buddy from work."

I glanced back at the car.

"About muffins?" I asked.

Shane frowned, confused. "What?"

"Nothing. Never mind." I tossed another glare at the Munsters and went inside like he asked, leaving the front door open.

Then I went straight to the kitchen window, one of those trailer bay style ones, and pulled down the blinds a little. Shane leaned into the car window and Mrs. Cryptkeeper slid something into his palm.

Dumbass.

My stomach clenched, but I kept watch until the car pulled away, and then I scrambled over to the couch and waited as nonchalantly as possible.

Shane pulled open the screen door and stomped his dusty boots on the deck.

"So what was that about?" I asked, spinning a lighter in my hand.

"Work stuff," he said, stepping in and closing the door. "I told you."

"Everything okay?"

"Yeah." He sat down and unlaced his boots. "Why wouldn't it be?"

"Well, I mean, are you calling off again tonight?"

He grinned and stood up. "Hey, it's my job to worry about you, not the other way around, remember?"

He ruffled my hair on his way down the hall, and when he shut the bathroom door, I crept down after him.

I put my ear against the wood, heard clacking and scraping, a snort and a sniffle, and my heart sank.

Chapter Fifteen

Zeke and I ditched school after the lunch bell to go smoke. We drove up to the old mines to stay away from any cops, even though it'd been gloomy all day and the dirt road was mostly mud and puddles. We parked in front of the schoolhouse steps, kept the doors closed, and decided to hotbox the car.

"You think he just lost it or what?" Zeke asked, passing me the joint.

"I dunno. I guess so." I took a hit, snorted and coughed. "His mom was a fucking terror, man."

He took the joint back. "He just didn't seem like the type, you know?"

"Yeah," I said, looking down at a little scar on my palm. "I know."

"It's the curse, man. I'm telling you." He handed the joint back, and I thought about what Denny had said about the tunnel, about how it had made his mom worse, but I kept my mouth shut.

"Fucking sucks," he said. "He was a funny guy."

"Yeah, he was." I took a hit, passed the joint back, and changed the subject. "I thought you were quitting this shit?"

Zeke took the joint between two fingers and looked down at it. "Man, I'm trying." Then he sucked on it like it pissed him off.

A small pickup truck came down the road through the drizzle and pulled up next to us. I caught sight of Jimmy Bannon in his blue and gold letterman jacket and some chick with him on the passenger side.

Zeke and I made some lewd jokes to ourselves and honked the horn a few times, and after a few minutes Jimmy opened the truck door with a sheepish grin and made his way over.

I stopped laughing and hit Zeke's chest and he hid the joint in the ashtray. No one ever got high with Jimmy. I thought my weed demons were bad, but this guy would turn into a puddle of tears and start in with all kinds of psychobabble bullshit about his fucked up childhood.

I rolled down my window and Jimmy rested an arm on the roof and leaned in.

"Yo, what's up?" he asked.

"Nothing man, just chillin," I said.

"Who's the babe," Zeke asked, grinning.

Jimmy blushed. "You all got an extra lighter?"

I reached into my jeans and handed him mine.

"So did you guys hear?" he asked.

Zeke turned down the radio. "Hear what?"

"They found Gavin and his sister dead in their pool last night."

"You're kidding," I said.

"Yeah, man. You know Derek? The quarterback, tall guy, used to date Sarah—"

"Yeah, I know who he is," I said, cutting Jimmy off. When he wasn't high, he just rambled about stupid shit.

"Yeah, well, he lives next door to Gavin, and he said he heard the screaming this morning. So he looked out his window and there was Gavin and Brenda, floating upside down in the water, their heads just slowly bumping up against each other where that filter box thingy is." He shook his head. "Bump, bump, bump, all dead. Their mom found them. How crazy is that?"

Zeke let out a whistle. "Damn, dude." He put his hands over his head, leaned back, and looked at me. "Do dead bodies float? I thought they sunk."

I ignored him. "What the fuck happened?" I asked Jimmy.

"Dunno. Some kind of accident, I guess. Weird thing was that they were in their regular clothes." He let that sink in for a minute and then hit the roof of the car with his palm. I jumped.

"Anyway, thanks, dudes." The sprinkles had gotten heavier, fat little drops hitting the windshield, and he hurried off back to his truck.

"*Dude,*" Zeke said as I rolled up the window.

"Yeah." I couldn't say anything else, not with the knot of dread in my gut. I sat back and stared at the schoolhouse steps, the raindrops staining the concrete dark in splattered patches.

"What the fuck were they swimming for?" Zeke asked. "It was cold as shit last night."

He looked at me for the answer and all I could manage was a shrug, because Gavin was walking around in my brain, running his fingers over the brick wall of my skull.

"Hey, you know Leslie Phillips?"

I looked over at him and frowned. "Who the fuck is Leslie Phillips?"

"This little chubby eighth grader that lives a few houses down from me."

"What about her?"

"She fucking stabbed some chick Saturday night at a sleepover. Can you believe that?" Sirens went off in the distance and Zeke twirled his finger in the air. "It's that fucking shit right there that gets to people."

"Yeah," I mumbled again. "Tell me about it."

He started the car, and I stared out through the hazy windshield at the ruins of the mining camp. "It's the curse of the ley lines," I muttered. Something about that struck me funny as hell and I started to laugh. Which I guess at the time was better than crying.

"You're high as shit, man," Zeke said, and then he was busting up too.

We were still a barrel of laughs as we came back into town, right until we got to Denny's street and saw the police cars and crime tape.

Zeke stopped the car on the corner and we watched the hustle and bustle of wet rain slickers and police dogs yanking on their chains for a minute.

I wiped my nose and Zeke looked over at me. "You okay, bro?"

I crossed my arms and nodded. "Yeah," I lied. I pictured Denny coming out of his house, waving a hand at us, and then coming over and saying, *Holy shit, dude. Did you hear what happened? Fucking cuh-ra-zee!*

And then me saying, *Man, chill out. You just fucking killed your mom, yo.*

Zeke sighed next to me and put the car back in drive. "Let's get outta here, dude. Go downtown and play some pool or something."

By the time the sun had set Zeke, Charlie, and I were standing in a doorway on Main, wasted as hell, and sharing a bottle of Green Apple Sour. Nasty stuff, but take what you can get, right?

Zeke set the empty bottle in the corner next to the rest and pulled out his hacky sack.

"You up for it?" he asked.

I snorted, then pushed myself off the ground, a little unsteady on my feet, and stumbled into Berm Hall.

"You fucking cocksucker," he said, shoving me to the side. "You want some of this?"

Berm's real name was Bertram, and he was a fucking tank. In seventh grade, he'd already had a full-on beard. Fuck no, I didn't want a piece of him.

"Sorry man, just a little tipsy," I said. Charlie stood up behind me, just in case. Getting prepared to use some of that Vietnam mojo on my behalf. I gave Berm my winningest grin.

Bertram's mad dog scowl broke into an alligator smile. "Hey! No worries, dude." He slapped me on the back. "Chill out. We're cool."

I nodded, surprised and relieved, and waved like a nerd as he headed back down the sidewalk. "Bye, Berm!" I yelled.

"See that?" I said, turning to Zeke with a buzzed grin. The kind you have when your lips feel numb and your brain says *Don't stop*. "I *totally* made him back down."

Zeke laughed and bounced the hacky sack on his heel. "Yeah, whatever, bro. You're the man."

But it wasn't two minutes later that the crowds started shouting *Fight! Fight! Fight!* and the three of us ran over to see what was going on.

Under the blue lights of Comet's, Berm was facing off with some kid— not anyone I knew, but I'd seen him in school before. Some clean cut cowboy. New in town. Fresh meat. And he had the height on Berm if not the muscle, and so after a minute of squaring off, the kid used his reach to sock Berm right in the nose.

Berm's head jerked back, and the kid grinned with victory. But only for a second. Berm charged like a bull and bum rushed him right into the wall. The kids head snapped back and hit the bricks and Berm started pummeling him in the gut. The kid came back up and swung again, but Berm grabbed him by the hair and bashed the back of his head into the wall. With the first hit, the crowd went into a shocked silence, and the kid tried to make one more clumsy swing, and then we all heard — and would never in our lives forget — the *thud, thud, splat* of cowboy's skull cracking open as Berm slammed it into the bricks over and over.

When he let go, the kid collapsed to the sidewalk, blood and grey matter and cerebral fluid sliding down the wall with him.

A girl screamed, high-pitched and shrill, and then the streets were in chaos.

I bent over and threw up all over my shoes. The stringy phlegm hanging from my lips reminded me of Cowboy's brains dangling from the wall and I threw up all over again as the crowd jostled me, their bodies screaming and shoving past me, wailing through Main long before the police sirens. I choked on my spit, my eyeballs wanting to pop out of my head and shadows crawling in and out of my vision. I looked up to see Berm staring at the bloody wall in a daze. Next thing I knew, Charlie was grabbing my arm and pulling me away and then we were in Zeke's car, screeching out of the alley and flying past the cops.

Chapter Sixteen

It started raining again by the time we pulled up to Charlie's place and, with our coats over our heads, we jogged up the steps just as the thunder started rolling in.

Charlie shut the door and flipped the switch on.

He lived in the caretaker's cottage on the Catholic church grounds, had been since he returned home from the war, getting free room and board for his labor and social security for his disabilities. It was a little studio place, maybe two cells wide, with a bed to the left of the door and two armchairs to the right, and a kitchenette and bathroom up a step in the back.

The thunderstorm outside made it a cozy place, especially since whoever had furnished it those many years ago had had a feminine touch. Rose-patterned ruffled curtains on the windows, throw pillows on the bed, lace lamps on the bedside tables. The walls were something else though, fully decorated in record albums, with squares like Fleetwood Mac, Lynyrd Skynyrd, and Iron Butterfly taking up every spare inch.

On the table between the two chairs was a terrarium full of snails.

"What's this?" I asked, wiping my nose and sitting down. My hands were still shaking.

"I'm raising 'em. You guys want some hot cocoa?"

"Yeah. Thanks. What do you mean raising them?"

Charlie had gone up the step into the kitchen. "For profit," he called back.

Zeke settled into the chair next to me and ran a hand over his braids. "Who buys snails?"

Charlie got the kettle going and came back with a spray bottle. "Lots of people," he said, misting the terrarium. "Restaurants, fishermen, gardeners."

"Oh." I sat back, and we all tried to think of something to say. It was one thing when your parents came home and told you the story about some woman they got transferred in who'd eaten her kid's face off, or when riots happened and the news said a mob of prisoners decapitated some dude's dad. But this shit was happening *to us*. Downtown. At home. The end of the road was getting closer and closer.

We stared at the snails and listened to the rain hitting the side of the house, lost in our own thoughts, until the teakettle started to whistle. Charlie pulled himself up off the bed and came back a second later with two mugs. "I put a sprinkle of cinnamon in it for you guys," he said.

"Thanks, man."

He sat on the bed criss-cross applesauce and sighed. "You okay, dudes?" he asked.

"Yeah," I said as the rain pattered outside. I held the mug in both hands and looked back and forth between the two. "What the fuck *was* that tonight, man?"

Zeke leaned back and ran a hand through his hair. "Holy shit, right?"

I shook my head and swallowed down the cocoa to wash the bile from my throat. "Fucking crazy thing is that was almost *me*," I said, pulling out a smoke. "One wrong word and he could have smashed in *my* head." My hand was still shaking as I lit the cigarette.

The three of us stared at nothing and tried to ignore the *thud, thud, splat* echoing in our brains.

"Paper this morning said a woman cut off her husband's hands." Charlie scratched his jaw. "Been some weird shit going on lately."

"Yeah," I scoffed. "You could say that."

"This whole fucking *town* is weird. Bad energy." Zeke said. Then he took a sip of cocoa with his pinky sticking out. I stared at him, thinking the whole thing was too fucking surreal.

"I took some 'shrooms the other night and I saw people out in the field," Charlie said.

Zeke glanced at me. "Your old Nam buddies again, Char?"

The thunder rumbled as Charlie leaned forward and handed me the box that held his pipe and weed.

I waved my hand at it. "Not tonight, man."

He handed it to Zeke, who took it gladly. "Not my buddies," Charlie said, a far off look in his eyes. "Just people. Coming up out of the dirt.

Like the Viet Cong used to."

Charlie wouldn't hurt a fly, I knew that. But Corporal Charles Kincaid was a different matter. Zeke and I had talked about it before, the possibility of flashbacks, especially with all that acid he'd dropped, and so I tapped the side of his shoe with my own. He tapped it back, (*I know*), and took a hit.

"Vortex of weird," Zeke said.

"You know you're in Stewartville when weird is normal," I said back.

Charlie reached up and pulled his medicine bag out from under his shirt. "Been getting worse though, hasn't it?" he asked, holding onto the necklace.

Zeke's little braids flopped as he shrugged. "Can it really *get* worse?"

I sucked in my lips and thought of Shane. Yeah, things could get worse.

"And can you believe Denny did that shit to his mom?" Zeke said, quiet now.

I took a drag and shook my head. "That was different, man." I scratched the side of my nose with the side of my thumb, thinking about those shadows, while the smoke got into my eye. Every time someone mentioned Denny, I had to fight back this vision of him straddling her on the basement floor, his face twisted in psychotic rage, the brick smashing down, down down…

"His mom was nuts," I said.

Charlie and Zeke looked at me but didn't say a word, and the room slowly started to spin.

"I'm gonna hit the john," I said, standing up slowly. I tried not to wobble up the single stair, and when I hit the door, I leaned on the knob and fell to my knees inside the tiny white bathroom.

The cocoa hadn't mixed well with whatever Apple Sour remained and it was coming up out of my gut in nasty heaves that left you swearing you'd never drink again. Halfway through my worship of the porcelain god, Charles threw on some Inagodadavida and the room pulsed with the beat, making me gag once or twice more.

Finally, I sat back and leaned my head against the white-tiled wall, clammy, tired and still half drunk.

Charlie's voice came through the thin white door, murmuring just under the music. "I think it's that tunnel, man."

"For real. Some weird shit has been happening ever since his boy found it." Zeke said.

"Oh, come on," I said to the wall across from me. I tried to pull myself up, holding onto the lip of the pedestal sink, and gave up as the room spun.

"I think they found it when they started mining in those mountains," Charlie said.

I slid down the wall and curled up on the bathroom floor, letting the cool porcelain touch my hot cheek. There was a pube three inches from my face but I didn't care. Okay, I cared a little. I tried to blow it further away, got lightheaded and sick all over again, and had to pull myself back up to the toilet.

"They unleashed it, and the evil came seeping out from deep in the ground."

I couldn't tell if it was Zeke or Charlie or someone else talking now, and then all I heard was gagging.

"... burning down the schoolhouse."

I coughed. Vomit went up my nose and a tear or two dropped into that brown, bubbling toilet bowl.

"... damn fools built that prison right up next to the mountain. Like having pigs in a pen."

I laid my arms over the toilet seat and rested my head on them as the wind howled outside. The cottage wasn't feeling all that cozy anymore and the stark little shitter wasn't helping my claustrophobia any either.

After a while, the music stopped and Zeke coughed. "So what do you think happened with Berm and Gavin?" he asked.

I lifted my head and snapped out an answer. "They didn't have anything to do with that tun—" And just like that, I realized my gut had me lying about Gavin in the AV room, running his hands over the bricks. Weirdness.

"What?" Zeke called.

I pulled myself up and looked in the mirror. "Nothing," I called back, as my vision darkened and then returned. I washed my face off, opened the door, and carefully walked back to my chair. "It's all just stupid ghost stories," I said, pulling out a cigarette but forgetting to light it. "There's nothing evil underground."

"So there's nothing weird about your buddy finding an underground tunnel in his basement and then killing his mom a couple of days later?" Zeke asked.

"Those tunnels were for the KKK," I reminded him.

Zeke scoffed. "Yeah, the KKK. Well-known for their positive and loving contributions to society." He wiggled the pipe at me. "You're just proving my point, man."

Charlie stood up like a knife cutting through the tension. "You all want some more cocoa?"

"Nah, man," I said, sitting back and putting my hands on my knees. I looked over at Zeke. "We should probably be getting out of here."

Zeke shook his head. "I'm way too high to drive, bro, and you're a fucking mess," he said. "Plus, it's raining fucking cats and dogs out there."

"Then can we drop it, at least?" I asked, curling up on the seat. "There's been enough weird shit tonight."

"Well, shit, man. Sure." Charlie walked to a box of records and began going through the albums. "Let me put on some more music and we'll just chill. Get some good vibes going."

I sighed and set my head back against the chair as the music began pulsing against the cottage walls again. Then I stuck my hand out towards Zeke. Without a word, he dropped the pipe into it and as I got high, I watched the snails leave a trail of slime up the terrarium walls.

Chapter Seventeen

The next morning Zeke and I swapped shirts and headed to school, late as all hell, making it just in time for lunch.

Funny thing about the prison and the school: they used the same food vendors. The lunch lady slapped ground beef gruel onto my tray and then gave me a little white bowl of green beans and an apple for dessert.

The lunchroom was practically a zoo which was normal I guess. What wasn't normal was half the floor sloping down towards oblivion and kids having to hold their trays on the table. But the new underground Super Max was being built, and that took up most of the town's resources. In time, they said.

I sat down with some guys I knew, over on the level side. Frank was down at the end talking to one of the mommy crew. She had to be about six months pregnant and was wearing this shirt that said, "Break In Case of Emergency," which had a condom sewn into a clear plastic pocket. Guess she liked the irony.

"Come on," Frank was saying. "Just a little dance. You know I have a pregnancy fetish."

Fucking Frank. I shook my head and shoveled ground beef into my mouth as the chick laughed and rubbed her belly.

"Jonny is gonna kick your ass when he gets out," she teased.

"Jonny ain't interested in women, babe." He stood up and ran a hand down her arm. "Not for the next 18 months, anyway."

That soured her mood. She slapped his hand away, waddled off, and he and the other guys started busting up.

I stacked my empty tray by the trashcans and then bumped into this chick Jenny in the hall. We went out to her car to toke a bit in the dirt student parking lot.

She was a trip, all into that earth spirituality, Wiccan Reiki crap. As soon as we got into the car, she started reading my aura.

"Yellow," she said. "With a hint of purple at the edges."

"What does that mean?"

"It means you're analytical, observant. A loner prone to mental health disorders."

I took the pipe from her ring-encrusted fingers. "That doesn't sound like me at all. And what's the purple?"

She tossed her blonde hair to one side and straightened the dream catcher hanging from the mirror. "Psychic, intuitive, philosophical."

"Huh," I said, all philosophical and shit.

"Now do me."

She sat back against the window and pursed her lips and batted her eyes. She should have been in pageants, but she dressed like a witch instead. Black skirt, black blouse, black boots.

"Uh… Purple?" I guessed.

She grinned and slapped my arm. "Yes! See you do have some of that in you. I knew it."

We took a few more hits and then I gave her the cashed bowl.

"Hey, you know anything about ley lines?" I asked.

"What?"

"This dude I know thinks Stewartville is fucked up because there's, like, this dark vortex that feeds on the negative energy here." I shrugged. "Or something."

She took the bowl back. "Oh, you mean like a *tulpa*?"

"A what now?"

"It's a thought form, generated by energy and emotions, and if it becomes strong enough, it can manifest as an actual being." She sat back and put her hands in her lap. "Wow. That actually makes *total* sense," she said to herself.

As I listened to her, the words *thought form, emotion*, and *manifest* swirled in my mind like a black, grasping cloud.

"So… you think that's what it is or what?" I asked.

"I fucking do *now*," she said, bending back through the seats to grab a colored, woven bag. She pulled it forward, plopped it on her lap, and started digging through it.

"Think about it," she said. "Think about how much anger and violence must be generated in there. That *emanates* from there. Until…"

And I thought about it, those prisons out in the field rushing to the forefront of my mind with a swirling mass of locusts above.

She pulled a sage stick out of the bag and lit it.

"What are you doing?"

"Cleansing the space."

The stick began to smolder, and I wrinkled my nose at the sharp smoke.

"Until what?" I asked.

"What?"

"You said emanating from the prisons until."

"Oh," She pulled a tape out of the console and popped it into the cassette player. Bob Marley. For the good vibes, I guess. "Well, until it becomes the demon of Stewartville, no longer just a product of our thoughts, but able to change our thoughts. Darken them, you know?"

I nodded. "Yeah. I think I know what you mean." I cleared my throat. "So it couldn't be unleashed? Like from a tunnel?"

"I mean, no. Not really. But it could probably feed off of whatever was *in* a tunnel."

The bell rang, its peal thinning as it reached us.

Chapter Eighteen

I sat in the AV room and stared over the table at the empty chair across from me while I spun my lighter.

I didn't want to be alone, because once again I felt less alone than I would have liked. And not just because of the weight of emptiness in the chair, but because there was also something behind me, a shadowy guilt at the thought of Shane and Nana. It felt like I'd been away from home for weeks and not just a single night.

Luckily it wasn't but a second later that the door opened behind me and I looked over my shoulder, happy for the break in silence.

"Hi," Ms. Alvarez said. Her heels clicked along the floor as she carried a box to the table. "By yourself today?"

She looked hot as always, and the potential in her words for a few thousand different porno scenarios ran through my mind in the space of a millisecond.

"Yeah," I said, clearing my throat. "Denny and Gavin—Yeah, it's just me."

"Oh. That's right. I'm so sorry." She set the box down and then came around to my side and sat on the edge of the table. Her lace bra peeked out from her silk blouse and I swallowed and looked away.

"How are you?" she asked softly, her breath smelling like mints.

Damn. I couldn't think. I cleared my throat and kept my eyes averted. "I'm okay," I said.

Ms. Alvarez put her hand on my shoulder and her French tips tickled my neck as she ran her thumb across my collarbone. That pushed Denny, Gavin and Nana right out of my mind, which made me feel like a dick but, damn, I couldn't help being seventeen you know?

"How about you do me a favor?" she asked.

Bow-chicka-wow-wow. I tried not to smile at the thought and there was no way I could make eye contact with her now.

"Sure," I said, and my voice fucking cracked. I cleared my throat as my face grew hot.

She sat back, and I put my hands in my lap, hiding the evidence of any sinful ideas I might have had.

"I have some boxes outside the door; why don't you put them away for me and then get out of here?"

"Seriously?" I looked up at her then, just to make sure she wasn't pulling my leg.

"Yeah. You don't need to be in this depressing room all by yourself." She stood up, rested her hand on my shoulder again and winked. "Just stay out of trouble, okay?"

There were five boxes outside the door, small and light enough so that a few minutes later I was picking up the last one. I carried it over to the farthest shelf and bent down to slide it onto the bottom shelf and that's how I noticed that three bricks were missing from the wall.

It only took a second to realize that it was the same spot where Gavin had been fucking around and as soon as I did the light above me buzzed, flickered, and went out.

"Fuck," I whispered in that way people do when they're alone in a dark place and need to scare away the void.

I stood up and reached into my pocket and pulled out the lighter. It clicked and sparked in the dark but wouldn't catch.

"Come on, motherfucker," I hissed. I flicked it a few more times and finally the flame caught and quivered, yellow and blue surrounded by black.

The wall was barely visible in the dim light. And maybe it was a trick of the shadows flickering over it, but from where I stood I could see holes all throughout the wall. The black gaps between the bricks thick and untouched by the light. Then, from the corner of my eye, I saw a whisper of movement in one.

White fingertips were spider-walking their way along the top of the bricks, like a blind person trying to see.

The lighter went out as I jumped back. I tripped over my own feet and fell to the floor, hard, then scuttled backwards in the dark until I hit the table. I grabbed onto it, scrambled up, and ran for the door. The knob wouldn't turn.

My mind raced a mile minute about how I didn't want to be one of those dumb ass people in the movies— the kind that can't fucking turn a doorknob to save their fucking lives — but the sweat on my palms had me fumbling, anyway.

But I just fucking knew that thing was climbing out of the wall, crawling towards me, those fingers about to reach out and grab me.

Just as I felt it whisper against my leg, the knob turned and I flew out the door, hauling ass through the auditorium, tripping and scrambling up the aisle.

I burst out into the empty hall, slammed the door behind me, slid down it, and took in the smell of applesauce and disinfectant with gulping breaths. I lifted the front of my shirt and wiped the sweat pouring down my face.

"You doing okay?"

The shirt fell, and I looked up at Mr. Anders standing above me.

He cocked his bald head and studied me for a minute. "You got a sec to come talk to me?"

I cleared my throat and pushed myself up. "Sure," I said. I was out in the light now, out in the normal open hallway of school and that's when I realized: *Fuck, I'm high.*

I followed him to his office, and he motioned for me to have a seat in front of his desk. Then he walked around and settled into the chair across from me, which creaked and dipped under his weight. I sucked in my lips and looked around, hoping that I seemed as chill as possible.

His office décor was all in teals, I guess to make it more soothing, but it reminded me of an old lady's house I'd been to once. Especially with all the plastic plants that covered his file cabinets.

"How've you been?" he asked, clasping his hands over his stomach. The tie resting on his thin white shirt bunched under his hands and he unclasped them to straighten it out, while the light from the window shone from behind him on his bald dome. Fucking scum bag. I wanted to call him out on Camille, but I kept my mouth shut and shrugged in answer.

"Have you given any thought to what you'll do after graduation?" He started rocking in the chair, ever so slightly.

"No," I said, realizing just then that I'd left my bag in the AV room. "Not really."

"College, trade school, career?"

I settled back and clasped my hands over my stomach. I'd heard of mirroring once and while I had no clue if it worked, I was high and willing to try anything to look normal.

"I don't know," I said. "I guess I'll probably just work at the cement plant with my brother."

"You're a bright kid. Don't sell yourself short."

I looked him dead in the eyes, forgetting to act normal. "Is there something wrong with the cement plant?" I asked.

He cleared his throat and smoothed the few strands of hair he had left on his head. "No. Of course, there's nothing *wrong* with it. But what are your dreams? Everyone should have a passion."

I stretched my legs out and looked down at my crossed arms. "Now that I think about it, I *have* always dreamed of being a guidance counselor."

His eyes narrowed and his chair stopped rocking. "Let's try to have a serious conversation," he said, clearing his throat.

"What do you mean? Is there something wrong with being a guidance counselor?"

He stared me down a minute. "Your brother, if I recall, had a scholarship to State."

I nodded.

He leaned *way* back and rested his hands on the armrests. "So how is everything? I noticed your attendance has been a little spotty. Are you having any problems at home?"

Danger, Will Robinson. I coughed and adjusted the jeans at my knee. "Yeah, it's all fine."

He rocked in his chair and watched me. "I'd hate to have to send out the truancy officer. You know it's an automatic thirty days at the juvenile detention."

"Yes sir. I understand. Just been some stuff going on."

"You mean the recent tragedies? How are you dealing with those?"

"OK, I guess."

He leaned forward and fiddled with the corner of his desk calendar. "You didn't seem okay out in the hall. "

"I mean, I guess you could say it's all been weighing on me a bit. Acting out is what you call it, right?"

Mr. Anders placed his chin on clasped hands. "That's right."

"It's just seems kind of weird, I guess. That all this stuff is happening? I mean, what do you make of it?" I stuck my tongue in my cheek and watched him as carefully as he was watching me.

"Son," he sighed. Then he leaned back and subtly tried to check his wristwatch and I knew then that I'd said all the right things. "When these things happen, they can trigger any underlying disturbances in others. Kids your age are very susceptible to being influenced. "

"Yeah, but influenced by what?"

"I'm sorry?"

I'd spoken without thinking and his eyes were on me like a laser again. "Nothing. Never mind."

He didn't speak for a minute, just rocked in his chair and watched me. At last he sat forward and began rearranging his desk.

"We'll have a school therapist here on Monday if you'd like to speak with her," he said. "There'll be an emotional support dog, too. That'll be nice, right?"

"Yeah. Sure. I like dogs."

He nodded and opened his mouth to speak again. I stood up.

"Well, I definitely appreciate the talk," I said. "But I better get going. Thanks, Mr. Anders."

He followed my lead and rose from his chair. "Just remember that my door is always open," he said. "Don't worry about things too much and try to enjoy your weekend."

He held the door for me and I headed past him through it.

"And start thinking about graduation, too," he remembered.

"Yes, sir." I was five steps down the hall when he popped his head back out and called out to the receptionist.

"Jenny." She looked up, her blonde hair brushing the collar of her black blouse. "Get ahold of the maintenance team and ask them to stop by," he said. "I think there are mice in the walls."

Chapter Nineteen

Shane was under the crawlspace when I got home, evidenced by the sound of metal clinking against metal, of soft thuds and hissing whispers.

"Hey!" I called out to him, passing his beat-up truck to stand in the weeds. It pissed me off, and he was gonna know about it. The noises stopped, but he didn't come out.

"Shane!"

And then his head poked out from under our trailer, his face dirty and wane and his jaw going a tweaker's mile. It's weird how addicts all look and behave alike. He'd been right. It ate your soul, and it had left him a caricature of a man, animated by muscle spasms and open sores.

"You okay?" I asked, losing my nerve at the pathetic sight of him.

"I'm fine," he said, his shoulders twitching. He'd lost about twenty pounds and definitely wouldn't be getting the chicks now. Not the good ones anyhow.

I took a step closer, deeper into the weeds. "What are you doing down there?"

His eyes widened—dramatically, comically—and he stuck a hand out, fingers splayed wide.

"Oh no no no, little dude," he said. "I'm taking care of it. You just go inside, okay?"

"Taking care of *what?*"

"Just go inside, man. Don't- don't- don't come down here, okay?"

"Yeah," I said. "OK."

I went inside but I couldn't listen to him down there anymore. Headphones on, I went into the kitchen to look for food and found an old can of hominy way back on the cupboard shelf.

I was halfway done with it when I noticed the letter to Shane sitting unopened on the kitchen counter. I guess I wasn't the only one not reading them anymore.

I tossed the can and looked out at the living room. "I'm tired of cleaning up after you, dipshit" I said in my best Shane voice.

Beer cans, plastic bowls, foilies, baggies — and oh great, a needle — all went into the trash bag. Then it was socks, shoes, pants.

I picked up a shirt from the end table and that's when I saw it. Our decrepit old answering machine blinking.

I dropped the clothes down on the recliner and pushed play.

There was nothing but quiet for a minute, then some rustling noises, and then someone panting and out of breath.

"Hey, dude. Are you there? Are you there?" Gavin's voice, hurried and frantic. "Come on man, pick up. Pick up, man." There was more panting, more rustling, and then soft sobs. "They're coming, dude. I can hear them scratching at the walls," he whispered. "Do you hear me? *They're fucking coming.*"

There was a click, and I thought that was the end of the message, but then I heard Shane.

"Hellooo?" his voice sang, in lilting falsetto. And then he giggled, high-pitched and insane, sounding just like a little kid, and sending a chill up my spine.

The message beeped.

"Shane!"

My head snapped towards Nana's door. The dim narrow hall seemed impossibly long, impossibly foreign, and I moved down it as if in a dream. I knocked on the door and opened it, feeling as if my real home were a million miles away.

"What do you need, Nana?"

"Where's Shane?" she spat. Her arms crossed over her fuzzy, zipped up nightgown. Her face wrinkled even deeper by her current temperament.

"He's busy, Nana."

She sat back on the pillows. "Well, get him in here. There's something scratching in the walls. A rat or something." She turned her head to me. "Get rid of it."

"What's wrong with you?" she spat again, because I'd just been standing there staring at her.

I gripped the doorknob in my right hand and the frame in my left. "Nana, it's aluminum siding. We don't have enough walls for the rats to live in."

"But it's *there*. You don't hear it?"

I lifted my eyes and looked around the room, listening and praying. But the only thing I heard was Shane beneath the floor.

"No, I don't hear anything."

She slapped her hands down on her lap. "But it's *there*," she whined.

Frustration got the better of me. I stepped into the room, snatched up her remote, and jammed down the volume button.

"Better?" I asked, nearly shouting.

She laid her head back and scowled at me. I immediately felt like a dick. "Sorry," I mumbled as I turned it back down.

Shane hit his head on the floor beneath us. Nana and I both glanced down.

"What's he *doing* down there?" she asked.

"Looking for rats, Nana."

I went back into the living room and started going through Shane's shit and, when I found the baggie full of powder in his work shirt, I took it into the bathroom. I'd been here before, staring in the same mirror with the same peeling wallpaper behind me, trying to get the balls to flush drugs down a calcified, brown toilet.

But the last time I'd done that, my mom had beaten my ass for it. I glanced at the scar over my eyebrow and then sat down on the toilet and bawled my eyes out.

Chapter Twenty

I stayed there for a while, head between my arms, staring at the little rusty air vent in the floor. The surrounding carpet had been cut, making it stand up in frayed little strands like a mossy green forest. At least that's what I'd pretended it was when I was little and would lay there with my army men, listening to mom and her friends partying in the living room.

I thought things would get better, not worse. I didn't expect great, because come on, this was Stewartville. But I'd thought with mom gone things would at least calm down enough for me to graduate. Maybe I'd work at the plant and get my own trailer, have Zeke and Charlie over once in a while. Maybe meet someone—

There was a knock out front.

"What's your brother doing under the trailer?" Camille asked as soon as I opened the door.

For fuck's sake. She'd dyed her hair red and was wearing a blue baby doll dress with black fishnet stockings and her old Doc Martens. She'd duct taped the holes in her shoes and had scribbled marker all over them. Song lyrics, anarchy symbols, hearts.

"What?" I asked, surprised and stalling for time.

"Something weird is going on over here," she said. "I've been watching."

"God, you freak, he's just working on something. Chill."

She crossed her arms and lifted her chin. "What's he working on?"

I put a hand on the screen door and leaned towards her, trying to be a little intimidating, a little cool, acting totally unnerved. "There's a cat or something under there, okay? Now skedaddle."

"Oh, bull-*shit*." She raised an eyebrow, totally not convinced. Fucking Camille.

"Look, I dunno, he just heard some scratching down there and he's looking into it." I watched to see how she'd react, wondering if maybe she'd heard it too.

"Oh, shit! Do y'all have squirrels?" She dropped her arms in disgust and looked at me with full on annoyance. So that was a no.

"What? *No,* we don't have squirrels."

"I swear to God, if y'all have a nest then you're paying for the—"

"Camille, it's not squirrels, okay?"

She narrowed her eyes at me. We stared at each other under the porch light until it became clear we were in a standoff, neither of us wanting to make the first move.

Finally, I took a step back and started to shut the door. "Well, if that was all— "

"He's tweaking balls, isn't he?" she asked.

There must have been a particularly bummed look on my face because her shoulders relaxed and her face softened. "Shit, dude. I'm sorry."

I looked away and wiped a hand under my nose. "Thanks. I'll talk to you later, Camille."

"Hey," she said before I could shut the door.

"What?" I asked, pulling it open once more.

"I mean, you can come over for a bit if you want. Mom's got people over but the coffee pots are going and we can hang out in my room." She shrugged and gave me a closed lipped smile. "We'll chill. Like old times."

I sighed and looked away. "I don't know."

She crossed her arms and shifted her weight. "You're still mad at me, aren't you?"

I ran my tongue over my teeth and nodded. "Yep," I said. "What you did was supremely fucked up."

She looked away, laughed under her breath, rolled her eyes. "I did you a favor, dude."

"A *favor?*" I opened the door wider and stepped out onto the porch. "You sold me aspirin and left me out there," I hissed.

She didn't back down. Instead, she waved a hand over at the crawl space and said: "Would you rather be doing *that?*"

I stared at her dumbfounded as the realization of what she was saying hit me like a ton of bricks. And then it pissed me off. "Are you insane?"

She shrugged. "At the time you wouldn't have taken no as an answer."

My face was hot with the new embarrassment. "Yeah, well, you still fucking left me out there," I said.

She wrinkled her nose. "Yeah, that was kinda messed up, but I *promise* I just wanted to ditch you so that one of them wouldn't give you the real stuff. It was Roy's idea to take your clothes."

"What the fuck?" I ran a hand through my hair. I couldn't believe her, man. She was nuts.

She reached out and patted my arm. "You can thank me later. See ya, loser." And then she was bouncing down the steps, the ends of her red bob brushing the white collar of her dress.

"Camille," I called.

She turned and shielded her eyes against the porch light. There were razor thin cuts on her pale wrist.

"Where'd you get that dress? You look like a Russian or something."

She grinned. "From ze Goodvill. You like?" She grabbed the hem and did a little sashay, then waved bye and crossed the lot.

I watched until she made it inside and then I shut the door and sat back down on the couch. Hands clasped between my knees, I stared at the light on the answering machine for a while and then I rose, went to the bedroom, and pulled my Walkman out from behind the bed. Music blaring, I crushed up some aspirin on the bathroom counter and put a baggie of it back in Shane's shirt pocket.

Chapter Twenty-One

I woke up and blinked at the sun coming in like a laser through the cracks of the towel I'd hung over my window. I pulled the headphones down around my neck, went to take a piss, and then stepped out into the living room to find Shane and his buddy hanging out on the sofa. There was a strip of foil and a straw on the coffee table in front of them, perfectly folded and charred with residual powder. And the place smelled like cat piss.

The buddy sat up straight when he saw me.

"Who the fuck is he?" he asked Shane.

"Chill, man. It's just my brother."

"Is he a snitch?"

My gut felt like someone had kicked it, but I ignored them and went to the fridge. It was still empty, nothing inside but rusted and stained plastic shelves.

"No, *Dwayne*, he's not a snitch. He's my fucking brother."

"He could still be wearing a fucking wire, man."

The room went quiet as my brother considered this.

"Hey, tell this dude you aren't wearing a wire."

Meth. Gotta love it.

Yeah, Dwayne, while I was in bed the cops came in and wired me up just to catch your ass. Paranoid, delusional motherfucker.

"I'm not wearing a wire," I repeated. I shut the fridge, went around the counter, and plopped down in the chair. I twiddled my fingers against the orange fabric of the armrest. I should have refused to answer on the principle of the matter, but no good came out of playing games with delusional junkies. I'd learned that the hard way.

"What's there to eat?" I asked.

"I don't know. Find something."

"I looked. There's nothing."

"Fuck. I don't know, dude. Find something." Shane bent his head over a small rock and scowled at it as he twisted it between his fingers and examined its surface.

I watched him quietly for a minute, sick to my stomach. He was apparently so deep in it he wasn't even bothering to hide it anymore.

Shane's buddy pulled his own rock out of a Sav-Mart bag and together they poured over the surface of the stones before gently setting them in a line along the scuffed coffee table. Then they grabbed another from the bag and repeated the process.

"What are you doing?" I asked, my voice coming out in a croak. The two looked up at me with dazed, glassy eyes and I was sure they'd forgotten I was there. Fucking assholes.

Shane scoffed. "Dude, there's so much you don't know." He held a pebble up between his fingers. "This, see this right here? It's a message, little dude."

"Yeah, man." His buddy carefully set his pebble down at the end of the line. "Prophecies. *The future.*"

Shane stood up and brought a stone over to me. "Look at it. Tell me what you see."

I raised my eyes to his bloodshot pupils, his rotten breath in my face, and took the pebble from between his trembling fingers.

It was a rock. Quartz and granite. Caked mud.

I stared down at it, hating him more in that moment than I ever had. My brother had turned into a fucking loser, a goddamn mother fucking idiot.

"Um," I said.

"You see it?"

"Yeah. Sure."

Shane took the rock back and cupped it carefully in his hands. "Whatever is down there is leaving me these."

"I thought you said it was just a cat or something down there."

Shane's buddy snorted. "*A cat.*"

"Yeah," I said. "I guess that *would* be pretty dumb, wouldn't it?" There was a flicker of self-awareness in his eyes and then it disappeared, lost in the haze and daze of fried egg brains.

"I gotta piss," Dwayne said, pushing himself up and adjusting his waistband over his gut.

I watched him walk down the hall and then leaned forward and searched Shane's face. "Dude. What's going on with you?"

He didn't glance up, he just kept spinning that damn rock between his fingers. "What do you mean?"

"Meth, man? I thought we had a deal."

His hand stilled, and he stared at the rock. "There's something under there, little dude." His voice was little more than a whisper and a hush fell over the living room, as thick and real as the dust swirling in the sunlight.

"No. There's not," I said. "When's the last time you slept, man?"

He brought his eyes to mine, and I saw Shane in them—the real Shane—down deep in the pupil like a figure at the end of a dark tunnel.

"Yes, there is. And it's fucking with my head, man. It won't leave me alone." He looked back at the rock, lost again, no longer lucid. "That's why I gotta do this shit. Figure it out."

Before I could say anything else, like, "Hey, maybe it's just the drugs?" Dwayne coughed and popped around the corner. He settled back down into the couch and stared me down.

"You sure you ain't wearing a wire, little dude?" he asked. "You gotta tell us or else it's entrapment."

"Don't call me that," I said, wishing the motherfucker would die on the spot. Aneurysm, spontaneous combustion, I didn't care. But I knew he was only there cause of me. Cause the shit in Shane's pocket hadn't worked.

"Why don't you get out of here, little dude?" Shane asked. "Go have some fun or something."

I pulled on the knees of my jeans and pushed myself out of the chair. "I'm gonna check on Nana," I said. "Someone has to." But they didn't care.

I went down the hall, rapped on the bedroom door, and found her snug in her bed and lost in soaps as always.

"You good?" I asked.

"What's Shane up to?"

"Busy with work and stuff." My stomach growled. "You hungry?"

She shrugged and held a crusty Kleenex up to her mouth, her eyes glued to the screen. I think she might have been crying into that thing since the seventies.

"I could eat," she said.

"I'll bring you back something in a bit, okay?"

There was a thunk beneath my feet, a thunk that rattled up my heels and into my knees. Dwayne must have left because Shane was back under the trailer, banging his head on the floorboards while he crawled around in the dirt.

"What is he *doing* down there?" Nana asked, looking at me as if asking for the first time.

"He just lost something, Nana. That's all."

I slipped Shane's keys off the hook and backed the truck out just as his head popped from around the skirting.

At the pawnshop, I traded in some CDs for a few bucks. After that, it was the Loaves 'n Fishes charity house, where I snagged bruised bananas, wilted squash, and some free books to sell at the used bookstore for more coin.

On the way to the grocery store, I pulled up to a red light next to a DOC bus. They blocked the windows with caging and I couldn't help wondering if mom was inside, staring back down at me.

The light turned green, and I left the bus rumbling down the road behind me.

Chapter Twenty-Two

My stomach grumbled as I walked up and down all eight aisles of the market with my Sav-Mart basket in hand. I would have killed for some of Shane's Stroganoff, but I filled the basket with Vienna sausages and ramen instead, hoping that Nana wouldn't mind too much.

It was harder to ignore the smell of body odor in line.

"So sad about that family," the woman behind me said to the cashier.

"Oh, yeah," the young girl replied. "He was my guidance counselor back in high school."

Beep, beep, beep, went the cans.

"Killed all of them," the woman behind me said, clucking her tongue. "Such a shame."

I looked between the two, my stomach clenching like I was about to have a massive shit.

"What—" I cleared my throat. "What happened?" I asked.

The woman in line looked me up and down like she wasn't sure if I'd just threatened to mug her or rape her.

"What happened?" I repeated. "With the family?"

The cashier smacked her gum and scanned a can. "Guidance counselor killed his wife and two young boys."

"Just chopped 'em up with an axe," the woman behind me said, speaking again to the cashier. She leaned forward towards her and said in hushed tones, "I heard he reorganized them. Into sculptures. With arms for heads and feet for hands."

A bald man twiddled his thumbs in my thoughts. *I think everyone should follow a passion.*

I grabbed my bags before I threw up all over the conveyor belt, stumbled past the windows full of blinding light and a fog of other people's smells, and made it to the double doors. They whooshed open, hitting me with fresh air. I wobbled over to the yellow curb and almost stepped off in front of a car.

The horn blared and snapped me out of it and as turned my head to follow the car, I spied the newspaper in the vending machine resting up against the faded blue bricks. The headline through the scratched glass caught my eye and so I dug the last quarter out of my pocket.

Before going home, I took a drive down Bell and stopped for a minute to look at Denny's house. A chill skipped up my spine as I double checked the paper.

Back at our lot, I turned the engine off and waited for Shane to come barging out the door, scream his head off at me, ground me for taking his truck. *Something.* But that was the old Shane, before the thing under the trailer began messing with his head.

I lit a cigarette and looked over at Camille sitting on her steps, cigarette at her lips, looking right back at me. I put my head back, took a drag, and didn't move again until I finished smoking the whole thing. I just needed five minutes. Five minutes of peace and quiet.

Smoke done, I grabbed the bag off the seat, and went inside to make food for Nana and give her her pills. Then I ate my noodles on the couch, bowl between my knees, droplets of broth splashing back onto the carpet as I read the paper on the coffee table. I set the bowl down, rubbed the spots out with the toe of my shoe, unplugged the answering machine, and grabbed my smokes.

I lit up on the porch. Camille was still outside and I headed over. She watched me approach, taking her own drag, squinting her eyes against the smoke.

"You wanna get outta here?" I asked, stopping at her feet. Across the lot Shep lounged in his pool and Blues travelled across the dusty air.

"Where do you wanna go?" she asked.

I sat down next to her and flicked my ash. "Anywhere that isn't Stewartville."

She leaned back on her palms and looked out at the fields. Her knees covered in striped tights, instead of dirt and band aids. I looked down at my own boots, replacing the dusty flip flops I'd worn.

And it was then that I realized all I wanted was to be a kid again. The years had been passing me by as I'd waited behind, irrationally thinking somehow time would circle back around and I could pick up right where I'd left off.

Camille pursed her lips and exhaled a thin stream of smoke. "You don't have money. A car."

I took a drag and shrugged. "We'll take Shane's truck."

"His registration is expired. I'm surprised you didn't get pulled over earlier."

"We'll hitchhike."

She laughed and bumped her shoulder into mine. "What do you have there, anyway?

I looked down at the answering machine. "You got a second to listen?"

Chapter Twenty-Three

I stepped into the shadowed living room, careful of the warped floors beneath the sagging, loose carpet. On the two dingy, now-beige couches—the kind that looked like they're upholstered with yarn—sat a group of people who looked up at us with wary, deadened eyes.

Some of them were missing their front teeth, some aged beyond their years, some looked like they'd stop trying years ago, and others trying just enough to still look clean.

The static filled, rabbit-eared TV was playing some crappy basic channel show, and a bong sat out on the coffee table next to an incense holder that swirled a steady stream of smoke into the air.

I'd spent so much time here as a kid that the smell was nostalgic. The cucumber peels left along the baseboards as an ant repellent, along with clumps of a borax and sugar mixture for the roaches, were pieces of my childhood. The same duct taped laundry basket was sitting on the stairs, the same carnival mirror pictures lined the wall. It was probably the same damn cockroach running across my shoe.

Time could stay still.

Camille led me through the memories to her bedroom, which was through a door on the left living room wall.

The pink sheet hung over her window and she still had the same posters on her wood-paneled wall, the kind you buy at the store and color in between the black velvet borders: Mushrooms, unicorns and rainbows. Those Trapper Keeper kind. I'd done the jungle jaguar one, in a crazy tie-dye scheme, which she'd hung right over her daybed.

"You kept it," I said.

She looked up at it as she sat on her mattress. "Who Fred? He's my buddy."

She stretched over to her nightstand and grabbed a crystal ashtray for me. It'd been mine for as long as I could remember, and it surprised me she still had that, too.

I took it and sat against the wall opposite her bed, answering machine in my lap.

"Been awhile since you've been over," she said.

I lit a cigarette, exhaled. "Yeah. Forever and a day."

"So what's going on?"

I plugged the machine in behind me and my finger hovered over the button. "Ready?"

She raised her eyebrows and nodded.

I pushed play.

Nothing.

"Shit, let me rewind it," I said.

She sighed and uncrossed her ankles as the machine whirred, came to a stop, and started to play.

You have a collect call from: Mom. *To accept this call, please press one.*
Beep
You have a collect call from: Mom. *To accept this call, please press one.*
Beep
You have a collect call from: Mom. *To accept this call, please press one.*
Beep
You have a collect call from: Mom. *To accept this call, please press one.*

Camille looked at me, understanding and sympathy written all over her face.

Beep

Hey, dude. Are you there? Are you there? Come on man, pick up. Pick up, man. They're coming, dude. They're coming.

Beep

She frowned. "That was Gavin?"

I nodded.

"*Dead* Gavin?"

"Yes, Camille."

"Why'd he call you?

"I dunno." I lifted my hands at her look. "*Really*. He was assigned to the books and we talked about Denny. That's all."

She was quiet for a minute, but she was also wiggling her foot around, agitated.

"All right. So who's coming?" she asked. "Ghosts? Vampires? Zombies? What are we talking about here?"

I picked at the denim strings at the hole in my knee. "Charlie and Zeke think it's some negative energy source in the earth." I shrugged at her look. "Yeah, I know. And Jenny Pinsko said it's a tulpa. Some kind of thought form thing."

"What do you think is going on?"

"I don't know. But take a look at this." I lifted my ass, pulled the newspaper out of my back pocket, and tossed it up on the bed.

She unfolded it. "It's just about the Historical Society,'" she said. She looked up at me. "What's the big deal?"

"See that house in the picture? The schoolteacher's old house? That's Denny's."

Her lips parted, and she looked at the paper with more interest. "The guy with a tunnel in his basement?"

"Yeah." I took a drag, flicked my ash in the crystal ashtray, and frowned at her. "How'd you know 'bout that?"

"Zeke told me."

So I told her everything. About finding the tunnel, about Gavin and Mr. Anders, about the scratching noise and Shane saying it was fucking with his head. At some point I got up off the floor and sat down on the bed next to her, and we laid back and looked at the white glow-in-the-dark stars she had pasted to her ceiling while we talked.

"I dunno," I said, turning my head toward her. "Maybe it's nothing."

She kicked the bottom of the bed with her shoe. "No," she said. "I definitely think something weird is going on."

"Like what?"

She lifted her left hand into a claw. "You got a thought form here, right?" Then she clawed at the air with her right. "And the ghosts of prisoners and miners in the tunnel here." She brought her hands together into a ball. "Put it all together and what do you have?"

I frowned. "What?"

"One big ass karmic retribution."

And there it was.

A heavy sense of doom filled me, cold and empty, the same feeling I got with the weed demons. A hopeless feeling that came from being wide awake, from when the bubble popped and the curtain was drawn back. I looked back at the ceiling and saw it for what it really was. The water spots. The smoke stains. The obvious poverty and despair of it all. And all I could think was, *What the fuck am I doing here?*, and it got harder to breathe.

"Can I tell you something?" I asked.

"Sure."

I took and deep breath, my hands rising and falling with my chest, and forced myself to speak.

Chapter Twenty-Four

I used to tell Camille everything, until that one summer when we'd been around thirteen, and had tagged along with Shane and some of his high school buddies up to Straw Mountain. They were going four-wheeling and we'd hopped out the back to sit on a dirt mound, share a soda, and watch the truck bounce over the trails, waiting with bated breath for a rollover or back flip. But after a while, Camille stood up and wiped the dirt from the bottom of her jean shorts.

"What are you doing?" I asked.

"I'm hot," she complained. She covered her eyes and gazed up at the mountain. Then she lifted her other hand and pointed at a rock shelf tucked back under an overhang. "Let's go sit in that shade up there."

So we'd climbed up, the shale stones slipping and crumbling beneath our feet, the scrub weeds scratching our shins. Out of breath, we collapsed on the rock ledge and fanned ourselves with nicked hands and dirty fingernails.

After a minute, I felt a draft on my back, where the sweat had made my shirt damp, and I turned around and held my hand up. "Hey, I think there's something back here," I said. A tan, jagged boulder was leaning up against the rock ledge and I gripped it with my fingertips and rolled it back. Sure enough, there was a hole, just large enough for a boy my size to squeeze through.

"Holy heck," Camille said. "You think it's a cave?"

"I'm pretty sure." Then, despite my better judgement, I tried to be a bad ass and impress her. "I'm gonna crawl in and check it out."

"Here," Camille said, pulling a little pink lighter out of her shorts and handing it to me.

I took it and got down on my stomach and slid myself in, like I was doing the worm or something. After a while, I'd started to think I'd made a bad decision. The lighter made it look like the tunnel opened up six inches ahead, but every time I'd scoot six inches up, it'd look like it was another six inches down. It wrapped me up in a rock burrito, and my elbows and ribs were hurting. I started to get where I couldn't even breathe.

"Camille!" I yelled, and my voice echoed down ahead of me into the void. To my surprise, a voice answered me from up ahead.

"Hey! Kid? Where are you?"

"I'm—I'm up here."

"Keep talking," he said. "I'll follow your voice."

"What do you want me to talk about?"

I heard rocks clattering but no answer.

"Hello?"

And then I saw the top of his head at the end of the hole, grey-blonde hair, frizzy and knotted.

I held my breath as he raised his chin and looked at me. "You're a goddamn lifesaver, you know that?"

"What—What are you doing down here?" I asked, noting the grey cotton at his shoulders.

"Don't worry about that, kiddo. Just help me get out."

It was difficult work turning around in that tunnel. And every time I'd lift my head and look behind me, that man's face would be right there smiling with stained crooked teeth that made me think of Hansel and Gretel and the oven.

The worst part was putting the lighter out when it got too hot and knowing he was in the darkness.,

"You're doing *great*, kid," he said.

When I finally hit open air, I could have cried. I scrambled out, wanting to get as far away as possible from that face, but instead of grabbing me, he stayed in, right at the edge.

"Hey. Is the coast clear, kid?"

Camille was down the hillside with Shane. They glanced up at me and she started waving her hands in the air.

"No."

"All right. Imma just gonna wait here then. You go on ahead."

As I turned to leave, the sirens started going off—*eeeerrroooo*, pause, *eeeerrroooo*—and the guy called out to me.

"Hey! Hey, kid. Don't mention this to anyone, okay?"

I nodded and then skipped down the hill as fast as I could back to Shane and Camille.

"You asshole," she said, slapping at me once I'd slid my way to the bottom. "You scared the hell out of me."

"Sorry," I mumbled, wiping myself off. I couldn't look at her, because all I saw and tasted were bones and rot, and when she stepped forward for a hug, I took a step back.

"Well, what did you see?" she asked, acting unfazed, but feeling it.

"Nothing. Just a little hollowed out part at the dead end."

"Why didn't you answer me? What took so long?"

"I just… I got claustrophobic is all. It was a tight space."

Life went on for the next few days and I didn't mention it. I figured the guy must have gotten away and fled town. But then two little girls had gone missing. A week later, they found them in an old house off the tracks with the inmate. Someone had bashed the girls' heads in and they found the inmate hanging from the light.

I went back up there and sealed the hole with rocks, and then I checked on 'em for a while when the sirens kept going off. But I told no one what happened. And I still couldn't.

Chapter Twenty-Five

"My mom's in prison because of me," I confessed on her bed. "I'm the one who turned her in."

Camille sat still for a moment, then turned and propped her head up on her hand. "Good," she said.

"Good?"

"She was a shitty person." She laid back again and scowled at the ceiling. "I wouldn't feel bad at all."

"Yeah, no. I don't feel bad for *her*," I said. "It's Shane."

Camille looked back at me and waited.

"He had a scholarship to State," I explained. It was my turn to look away at the ceiling, my face hot. "I didn't want him to go. I didn't want to be alone. With her."

Camille kicked her heels against the bed frame again. "And so he had to give up the scholarship and stay here to look after you."

Tears prickled behind my eyes. "I ruined his life, man."

"That's not true—"

"He's a tweaker in this shitty town, working at the cement plant, Camille. Hell yes, it's fucking true."

"No, your *mom* ruined his life," she said. "Just like she ruined Roy's."

"What are you talking about?"

"Oh, you didn't know?" She kicked the bed frame harder, faster. "Your mom's the one that got him hooked. Got him dealing. She was his supplier."

"Shit," I breathed. It was quiet for a long minute as her words sunk in.

"Is that why you were looking? Because you felt guilty about Shane?" she asked.

She meant the meth. I swallowed and scratched my nose. "Yeah," I lied, thinking of those two little girls.

She furrowed her brow and nodded. After a second she pursed her lips in that angry way she had. "Say it is a thought form. It's like that thing is fucking with people's heads, right? Making them become their worst fear."

"What?"

"Think about it. Denny killed his mom. Gavin and his sister died in the pool. Shane becomes a tweaker. It makes sense."

I scratched my cheek and thought it over. "I guess. But come on, you can't seriously think there's—"

Camille looked at me and something in her eyes shut me right the fuck up. "And what happens when it finds the wrong person?" she asked.

I frowned at her, confused. "What do you mean?"

"What if it finds someone to go on a killing spree? Someone who's gonna 'Donald Geist' the place. "

After she said that, it didn't feel like there were only two of us in the room anymore.

"Let's just go, Camille," I said. "Get the hell out of here. I can make it work."

Her feet stopped kicking around. "What about Steve?" she asked quietly.

"Shit, bring Steve. I don't care. We just need to get out of this town, Camille. Before it swallows us alive."

She blushed at that but I looked away and didn't think about why, because the knob was turning, and then there was Steve in the doorway, looking down at us.

"Hey man," he said. But what he really meant was, *Get the fuck off my girlfriend's bed.*

Camille and I sat up, feeling guilty for doing nothing.

"I figured you'd be with your buddy Zeke," he said.

"What do you mean?"

"You haven't heard?" Steve came in and leaned against the wall. "He's having a major freak out, man." He grinned. "His mom isn't getting out."

Oh, fuck.

I scrambled up and grabbed the answering machine, noticing something on the floor behind it. "Hey," I said to Camille, quickly pocketing it. "I'll talk to you later, all right?"

She nodded, her brown eyes worried, and I hurried out of the room, out of the house, and across the lot.

Chapter Twenty-Six

Zeke's was a small, grey house down on Third Street. I opened the chain-link gate and stepped through the dirt yard to knock on a bare wood front door that didn't even shut flush against the frame.

Charlie opened the door.

"Hey, man," I said, walking in. "Heard Zeke is freaking out?"

"Yeah, man. He's downstairs in the basement."

I went through to the kitchen and as soon as I saw that cracked door it was like déjà vu. It creaked as I opened it wider and looked down. The stairs came down almost right up on the opposite wall, and around the corner of them I could see the edges of light.

"Hey! Zeke!" I called from the top. "You in here?"

"Over here," he called back, his voice muffled around the corner.

The stairs were thin and steep and I took them carefully. They made the basement walls of lopsided bricks that had settled on a three-foot wall of dirt. The floor was a mixture of concrete and mud, and my boots squelched into the cool dampness.

I turned the corner and found him halfway inside the dirt wall, his feet sticking out. The bare light bulb swung over a pile of moist earth.

"What the fuck are you doing?"

"Hey, bro," he said from inside the hole, all casual like nothing was fucking weird about what he was doing. "You hear about my mom?"

I nodded, realized he couldn't see me, and cleared my throat. "Yeah, man. Look, I'm sorry. That really fucking sucks."

He grunted and a clod of dirt flew out the hole. "Yeah, well, I'm gonna end this shit once and for all."

A creepy, crawling feeling went over my scalp. "What do you mean?"

"You hear that scratching? It's in the walls, man."

"What is?"

"It."

"*It*, what?"

His feet moved out of the hole, then his legs, and then he had pulled himself out, his hair and face covered in soil.

"Come on. Who are you kidding, man?" He was down on his knees, his hands resting on his thighs. "That thing we saw at the mine."

"What thing? What the fuck are you talking about?"

"You, me, and Denny. Remember?"

A chill filled the room, and the shadows bounced along the walls as the light bulb swept back and forth on its chain.

"Dude. Come on. This is crazy."

Zeke shook his head. "I know we promised we wouldn't talk about it, but it's too late. It's fucking with us."

He lifted his hands to the wall and started pulling out more dirt around the edges.

"I don't know what you're talking about, man. For real."

"Pfft. Yeah, right! You were crying like a bitch in the backseat." He tossed more dirt aside. "You don't remember that?"

I knelt down next to him. "Look, why don't you just leave this shit alone for now, man? Let's go get some beer and go relax at the creek."

He wasn't listening. He just kept pulling at the dirt, so I rested a hand on his shoulder. "Dude, seriously. Knock it the fuck off."

He turned and looked at me. "What's your deal, man?"

"OK, say we *did* see something." I looked him dead in the eye. "If so, then it's not something we wanna fuck with, right?"

"Oh my god," he said, and I started to relax, thinking he saw reason. "Denny was fucking right about you. "

My shoulders went tense all over again. "What?"

"You're a fucking pussy, you know that?"

"For real? You're really gonna say that shit to me? What about Gavin, dude? Leslie Philips? Mr. Anders fucking chopping up his family and gluing them back together? I'm a *pussy* for not wanting to mess with any fucked up shit like that?"

He licked his lips like he was ready to unload when Charlie called down from the kitchen. "You dudes okay down there?"

It was enough to cut through the tension. Zeke ran his tongue over his teeth and looked back at the wall and the light bulb swayed above us.

"I don't know. Maybe you're right."

"Come on, dude. Let's just go upstairs and forget about it, man."

Zeke lifted himself up. "Yeah," he said, turning towards the stairs "OK."

"Hey," I said.

He turned back to look at me.

"It's gonna be okay, man."

"Yeah," he scoffed. "Just six more months and then we're outta here, bro. Gonna head to Iowa and live with my grandparents."

Once the three of us were upstairs together, I clapped my hands together and looked at Zeke and Charlie. "So, beer? I gotta pick up smokes anyway."

Charlie stretched and nodded. "Yeah man. Sounds good."

"Let me grab some change real quick," Zeke said.

We climbed into Shane's truck and headed up to the station. I parked across the street in the empty lot, just in case, what with the bad registration and all. Sirens went off in the distance. A slow and long wailing that always activated my lizard brain and made it think of danger and shelter.

I hopped out the truck and Zeke followed.

"Hey, let me get if for you, man."

"Are you sure?"

"Yeah, it's cool." He looked over at Charlie. "You need anything?"

Charlie shook his head, and I climbed back in.

I rolled down my window and lit a cigarette. Last one, nothing but loose leaf tobacco inside.

"So what happened?" I asked Charlie.

"A fight," he said. "Wasn't her fault. She got jumped. But she's getting assault charges and at least another six months."

"Damn." My heart sank. "That sucks, man. What was she supposed to do? Just take the punches?"

Charlie sucked on the joint. "They don't care, man." He handed me the joint, and I waved it off. "So anyway, Zeke ran into that Steve guy, they started talking, and he's been acting weird ever since."

"Damn, man." I looked at the cigarette between my fingers. The fine white paper made me think of pissed stained tighty-whities.

I weren't sick till I got here.

I pulled out the pentagram necklace from Camille's room.

"What's that?" Charlie asked.

"I'm not sure yet," I said, dangling it over my finger. "I've been thinking though, about the ley lines and stuff…"

"Yeah?"

"It's bullshit, right?"

He put a hand out for the smoke, took it from me, his cheeks sinking in as he took a drag.

"Like the shit we've seen, man," I said. "Berm bashing in that kid's skull? Denny. Yeah, well, that shit is scarier and more real than any damn vortex. The ghost stories just make all that shit a little easier to think about, right?"

He handed me back the cigarette and exhaled.

"Maybe that's how it traps you," he said. "You start thinking it's *normal.* But I *see* 'em, you know? The guys from my company? Sometimes I'll just be bopping down Main, doing my thang, and I'll glance in a window and there one of 'em is, staring back at me through the glass."

I didn't know what to say to that. "Crazy," is what I settled on.

"That ain't a ghost story, bud. And I been seeing other people, too. Every night they've been standing out in the field and stare at my house. "

"What do you think they want?" I asked, putting the necklace away.

"Well, I don't know. But I think one of 'em stole my boxers. And they also moved my rye bread. But hey man, the craziness keeps me sane. Good old Stewartville."

We fell quiet again, Charlie tripping out in his thoughts and me thinking about what was in my pocket.

I finished my cigarette and flicked it into the alley. "I'm gonna go find Zeke. You gonna be all right out here?"

"Oh yeah, I'm just fine."

I put a hand on his shoulder and, as I stepped out, I felt a gut thing. A nostalgia. I lifted my head and watched as Zeke made it to the front of the line and stepped up to the counter. I turned to say something about it to Charlie and the shot rang out, muffled through the glass.

I spun my head around. Zeke was still in front of the counter, a gun in hand. But the cashier wasn't there, a blood-stained wall in her place.

"Holy fuck," I shouted, louder the second time. "*Holy fuck!*"

"Get in and get the fuck out of here," Charlie said.

Customers ran out of the store. A woman dropped her milk jugs, the white stain splattered and spread on the dark pavement. They were screaming and crying and I could only stare at them in absolute shock.

It took my brain another minute to believe it was real. But it was all too real, and it was one of those things, one of those dreaded awful things that you wish you could take back but can't.

Charlie leaned across the seat. "We have to go, man!"

"But Zeke—"

"You can't do anything for him. Just get us the fuck out of here before we go down too." Sirens were wailing now.

I nodded, climbed into the truck, and as I turned the key, I met Zeke's dreadful, shocked eyes. As I threw the truck into gear he kissed his fingertips, raised them in the air, and brought the gun to his head.

"*Fuck!*" I shouted as the tires squealed out of the lot.

Cop cars flew by us a block or two down and we watched them pass without saying a word, keeping our eyes straight ahead. Sweat ran from my temples, my damp hands slid over the wheel, and I was pretty sure I would vomit.

So I pulled over at an old realty office, where litter cluttered the doorstep and dust cluttered the windows and took a few breaths with my head on the wheel.

"I'm gonna let you out here," I told Charlie. "I just need to get home. I'm sorry."

"It's cool." He opened the door. "The walk will clear my head."

"Yeah, man. I'll catch you later, okay?"

So fucking normal. Like our friend hadn't just shot his brains out after killing a clerk.

Charlie shut the door and waved at me. A few minutes later, I parked in front of the trailer.

I didn't want to cry. Wanted to hit something. So I started bashing the steering wheel, going off on it like I was throwing punches at the universe.

Six more months, man. That's all he had to wait.

Until something else fucked it up, until his hopes were fucking dashed again. Because that was life in mother fucking Stewartville, wasn't it?

Worn out, I left the truck, climbed the old wooden stairs, kicked the aquarium and smashed the glass, then opened the door and went into the kitchen.

I stood there for a minute, thinking about how the light was always orange in the trailer. A hazy, foggy, orange gloom first from the sun and then from the prisons. How, day and night, it clashed with our olive green countertops and scratched wood cabinets.

Then I went to the sink and threw up.

Chapter Twenty-Seven

The water washed the bile down the drain in swirling, phlegmy loops. I wiped my face with my shirt and my eyes landed on the letter.

It was thin, probably only had a sheet or two inside. I tapped it against my palm for a second and then took it with me outside.

I picked through the cigarette butts at the bottom of the stairs until I found a large one. The lighter flicked, and the smoke rose into my eyes as I held the cigarette with my lips and opened the envelope.

Inhale. Exhale.

Hey Sweetie,

I know you're not reading these but I'm your momma so I'm gonna keep writing you, anyway. Not that I've always been the best momma, and you have no idea how sorry I am for that. But no excuses. I'm done with those.

I guess you could say that when your own kid turns you in, that's a sign that shit ain't right with you. A wake-up call. And I said some things I never should have. But I'm not mad at you, baby, so don't you worry about that. It was a miracle of God, what you did. You're my guardian angel. You saved my life.

Our counselor told us that the hardest thing to do is usually the right thing to do and that made me think of you and my heart swelled with pride. You're so good, angel, even if you might not know it. So you just keep on doing those hard things and making the world a better place. No one else is gonna. And I promise you when I'm out, I'll be the momma you always should've had and you won't have to worry about a thing.

I love you.

Mom

P.S. Enclosed is a bracelet I made for you. I'll write again tomorrow. Sure would love to hear back from you.

I folded up the letter, flicked my ash into the weeds, and looked at the bracelet resting over my fingers. It was one of those friendship-braided things, neon pink and orange, something a ten-year-old would make.

Nana's voice cut through the walls of the trailer. "Shane?"

I sighed and stuck the bracelet in my pocket, put the letter in my inside coat pocket, and headed down the hall.

I knocked and cracked the door. "Nana? Shane's not here."

"My tape is finished," she said from the bed.

"You want me to rewind it?"

She looked up at me and it took a sec for it to dawn on me she was actually lucid. I squirmed under her gaze.

"What's wrong, honey?" she asked.

I swallowed, not trusting myself to speak, and just shook my head.

She patted the bed next to her. "Come sit with me for a bit."

I went around the foot of her bed, hitting rewind on my way past the VCR, and then climbed up next to her.

"Your momma used to like to come and lay down with me," she said. "No matter how old she got. Whenever she had a problem, all she wanted was just to crawl up next to me and lie her head on my shoulder."

I laid back on the pillow, keeping my boots hanging off the edge of the bed.

"She had a difficult time of it, she did. Straight-A student. Prom queen. But there was still a sadness about her. It was hard on her when her daddy died, you know? And then, of course, there was your own daddy."

I must have had a look on my face because she waved her hand. "Oh, I know she gave you some story. Doesn't want to talk about the truth, I guess. That was always her problem, bottling everything up. You're a lot like her, you know."

"Did you know my dad?"

"No, he never came around and she didn't speak of him much, even though he only lived right around the corner. He was a colored boy, you see, so I think she was embarrassed, worried I'd say something. What was his name? Herald, Carl, Charles. Well, I'm not sure, anymore. But she sure was heartbroken when it ended."

The VCR clicked to a stop.

"Your tape's done," I said after a second or two, my voice like a stranger's.

"Go ahead and push play then."

I climbed off the bed and started the tape, and she settled her shoulders back into the pillows and clasped her hands over her lap.

"Come lie back down, honey. Don't worry about a thing. Nana's here."

I walked back around the bed, kicked my boots off, and within minutes I fell asleep as the truck fired to life.

Chapter Twenty-Eight

"Shane! Shane! Shane!"

Nana's screams cut through the air. My eyes flew open, and it took a minute to orientate myself in her shadowy room. I turned my head and blinked back the fuzz. Nana was standing across the bed from me, a pistol in her hand.

I was wide awake then, and I sat up, slowly and carefully.

"Nana, what are you doing with that?" It must have been Pappy's. Why the fuck had we ever let her store shit in here?

"It's the scratching!" she cried. Her wild and teary eyes scanned the corners of the room. "Those people are trying to get in. They're trying to get my head."

"Nana, I promise. They're not." This didn't calm her, and she waved the pistol around just as dangerous as before. "I won't let them, Nana."

She looked at me, weighing my words, and then her eyes narrowed and she raised the pistol in her shaking, liver-spotted hand.

"You're helping them."

Oh, fuck me. I raised my hands and carefully stood. "Nana—"

"You're not getting my brain."

"I don't want your brain, Nana."

"Yes, you do. I heard you whispering about it. Scratching around under there, trying to get me. Why else are you in here?"

"Nana, I promise you. Please put the gun down."

Her finger moved on the trigger. Luckily, she was old, and slow, and shaky. By the time she fired I had already dropped beside the bed.

I looked up over my shoulder and saw the bullet hole through the paneling, a foot from where my head had been.

"Oh no," she breathed above me. "Oh, sweet Jesus, no."

I heard the gun cock, and I looked under the mattress at her bare, blue and white feet. "Nana, I'm fine!" I shouted. "I'm fine, Nana!"

But the shot rang out, anyway. I snapped my head away and even over the ringing in my ears I still heard her body thud to the ground. I squeezed my eyes shut, praying with everything I had, and after a few minutes I turned my head to look.

No, no, no, no, no.

It was like looking at five pounds of ground beef that someone had dropped on the floor.

My body seized and heaved into the fetal position. Vomit came out my nose and mouth onto the carpet beneath me. I lifted my head out of the puddle—tears, snot, and spit dangling into the bile—and tried to crawl my way out, stopping to vomit once or twice more.

Outside, Shane pulled back up in the truck and rage replaced my grief.

I had to crawl past Nana. There was no avoiding that. First, I saw her feet and, if I just pretended everything else was fine, it wasn't so bad. But the blood spreading through the green, mossy carpet made pretending impossible. I shuddered and dropped my head to sob for a second more. With a grimace, I reached out, grabbed the pistol laying beside her, and crawled my way down the hall to the front door.

The screen door whacked the side of the trailer. And there was Shane still sitting behind the wheel, sniffing a line off of his ID without a care in the fucking world. The wind flapped the blue tarp in the back of his truck and I saw a glimpse of something that made my stomach churn.

"*Shane!*"

He looked up at me and wiped his nose, his eyes widening as I raised the pistol.

"Get out!" I shouted, tears running down my face.

Shane put up one hand and slowly opened the car door with the other. "Whoa, little dude. What are you doing?"

My face collapsed and the snot and tears started mixing again. There we were, standing under the blue sky while someone's radio played the Eagles, just like it was any normal day. Except everything had changed.

"Nana's dead," I blubbered.

Shane's face twisted up in cracked out confusion. "What?"

"*Nana's dead!*" I screamed at him.

His head shook. "How? What?"

"Where *were* you?"

Shane took a step closer. "Look, little dude. I'm so sorry. You have no idea. Just put the gun down and we'll talk."

People were coming out to look at us now.

I straightened the pistol and looked him dead in the eye. "What's under the tarp?" I asked. He didn't move. "Show me!"

He nodded. "Hey, okay. Be cool," he said. He lifted the tarp and then softer he said, "There's something under the house--"

"No! Shut up! Shut up! Fuck you!"

He stood silent and stupid and I raised my arm to wipe my eyes. I'd been mad when I grabbed the gun. Mad and scared and heartbroken. But with it in my hand, with the weight pulling on my wrist, I felt surer than I ever had before.

"Don't shoot me, kiddo."

Oh, I wasn't going to shoot him. Nope. I was going to do one even better.

As I stared at the dynamite he'd stolen from the plant, all I could hear was Camille's voice in my head. *What happens if it gets to the wrong person?*

DOORS

Chapter Twenty-Nine

There might be three reasons to move to Stewartville but the natives, like myself, stayed because of just one: we'd lost the will to leave. Life here sucked the hope right out of us. Just like it'd done to Denny and just like it'd done to Zeke.

Sometimes it wasn't so bad. Sometimes you'd be hanging out with the guys — cruising up to the mines in an old Camaro, beer in hand and the music on — and you'd think "This is okay. This is all right." But it didn't matter what you did or who you were, nothing ever changed. Not really.

The door in the big house slammed closed as Camille stepped out onto the porch, arms wrapped around herself. She looked at us a minute, just another face in the growing crowd, and then with a deep breath she came over.

"What are you *doing?*" she hissed, staring at the gun in my hand.

"It's Shane," I told her. *Please don't think I'm nuts*, my eyes begged. "He's gonna Donald Geist the place. Look in the back of his truck."

She went up to the side of the bed and her eyes widened. "Holy cow," she breathed.

"What the hell are you talking about?" Shane asked.

I didn't have time to explain it to him. People would call the cops soon.

I went down the steps and waved the gun at him. "Get over on the deck," I said. "Away from the truck."

He stared at me but didn't move.

"Don't fuck with me, Shane," I warned. "I swear to God I'll shoot you in the fucking leg."

His face turned dark, but he nodded and slowly made his way over. I backed up, keeping myself out of arm's reach, until we had swapped positions.

Sirens wailed across town.

"Dude—" Shane took a step forward, and I raised the gun again.

"Don't even think about it."

I opened the door and glanced down, catching sight of the baggie on the seat. It was strawberry printed. Just like the ones Roy used. His trademark.

"I'll go with you," Camille said, her voice breaking through the puzzle.

I swallowed. Nodded. "Yeah. Okay," I said.

She climbed in and I rolled down the window. "I'm not mad at you, Shane," I called to him. "I know this isn't your fault. But I'm going to fix it, I promise."

I backed out and turned onto the main road, and Camille and I stayed quiet for a while. Both of us lost in our thoughts.

"So what's the plan?" she asked finally.

I turned down Pear, towards the Loaf N Jug. "Well," I ran a hand through my hair. "First, I need to get smokes, I guess."

She laughed and moved the hair blowing into her eyes. "Of course you do."

"And then we're going to Denny's." I glanced over at her. "Into that tunnel."

She took a deep breath. "Maybe that's—"

"Just trust me, Camille."

She swallowed. Nodded. "Yeah. Okay," she said.

We drove by the gas station, crime scene tape strewn across it like streamers at a party. Cops stood in groups. Still talking to reporters. Still cleaning up.

"What happened there?" she asked.

"Zeke shot the clerk and then blew his brains out."

I felt her eyes on me as I stared straight ahead. "Okay, *seriously?*" she asked. "What the fuck?" She fell back against the seat and let out a shaky breath. "Jesus Christ," she said. And then she sniffled. I looked over at her then, but she wiped a hand under her nose and turned her wet face to the window.

I took the highway and pulled into one of the many liquor stores that lit up the road. "You mind running in for me?" I asked, turning off the car under the red lights of the sign.

She sighed but stuck out her hand for the cash, anyway. It took her about five minutes, after getting the money, to come back and put a pack back in mine. While she was gone, I picked up the baggie, and folded it between my fingers lost in thought.

"Denny's now?" she asked.

I opened the pack, lit up and exhaled. I wouldn't be getting a lot of smokes after this. Not with where I was headed.

"I wanna stop by Charlie's real quick first," I said.

"Why?"

"Just to say bye. In case anything goes wrong."

"So you *do* think something will go wrong?"

I shrugged. "I'm blowing up the tunnels, Camille. So probably." I looked over at her, hand waiting on the gearshift. "Still wanna tag along?"

She pursed her lips and shook her head. Then with a sigh she raised and dropped her hand. "Sure. Why the hell not?" She turned, studied me, and then gave me a weary smile. "Someone needs to keep an eye on you, I guess."

Evening mass was already starting at the church and as we drove past slowly towards the dirt road, the men, women and children milled their way up to the door.

"If only they knew," Camille said. "Then they'd *really* be praying up a storm."

I flicked my cigarette ash out the window and took another drag, with no idea what the fuck I was actually doing. A minute later, the truck came to a stop at the cottage.

"Wait here," I told Camille.

I knocked. No answer. With prayers of my own, I turned the knob and stepped in.

Chapter Thirty

"What's wrong?" Camille asked.

I climbed in, dried my eyes on my sleeve, and shook my head. "Nothing," I answered, running a knuckle over my forehead before starting the truck. "I don't want to talk about it. Just…" The engine roared to life. "You're all I got left, okay?"

She sighed and nodded, but asked no more questions as we drove back through the field.

"You know," she said, looking out the window. The sun was setting and a haze of humidity settled above the fertilized soil. Sunflowers grew wild alongside the road and bent west. "Stewartville is kinda pretty in its own way."

"Yeah," I said, looking out at it with her. "I guess it is."

We drove for a few more blocks and then freaked about halfway to Denny's, when a cop stopped at a light two cars behind us.

"The registration," she said.

"The dynamite," I said.

I took the next right and watched through the rearview mirror as the cop went straight. My shoulders relaxed and my breath came back. I mean, not that I wasn't already expecting jail after this, but shit had to get done first.

The crime scene tape was still up at Denny's — just barely — the loose, ripped ends flapping in the breeze. And from the looks of things, they abandoned the place. Abandoned by the police. Abandoned by hope. Abandoned by me that last night, when I should have done more.

Abandoned by all but evil.

I didn't want to do this. I dreaded it, in fact. Tears of injustice stung my eyes. The injustice of finding myself in a situation I shouldn't have had to be in. And sure, I could leave. I could run. But the problem would still be there, right at my back. So, I had to do it, even though I knew there was nothing good waiting for me in that tunnel. I'd known it the minute we found it.

"Fuck," I hissed, dropping my head in my hand and squinting my eyes. Parked back in the alley with the engine off, I took a deep breath and then straightened up. "Come on," I said. "Let's just do this."

"Wait, what's the plan?" Camille asked.

"We're gonna blow it up."

A small smile lifted the corners of her mouth, like a meteor across the sky, here and then gone. "So, you said. But how?"

"I'm gonna blow up the entrance and the exits."

She turned in the seat and faced me. "And what's that gonna accomplish?"

I shrugged and looked at Denny's dark and waiting house. "It'll stop it."

"Stop what?"

I chewed on my lip. "Stop **It** from ever getting out again."

I didn't even like talking about it.

Her hand rose and then fell, defeated. Her sigh tickled the back of my neck.

"All right," she said. "Let's just do this."

We opened the car doors and stepped around to the bed of the truck. Even with Camille there, pulling out a bundle of sticks across the truck from me, I knew this was all on me alone. Fate. Destiny.

Karma.

In a way, I guess I'd been inside that tunnel since before the first draft had hit my fingers. And then, as soon as Denny and I had pulled those bricks out and opened it up, it had swallowed us all whole, so that there wasn't an entrance anymore, there was just an end.

Please, please, please, I prayed as I gathered the sticks and cradled them against my chest. *Please let this fucking work.*

I started thinking of that black hole, just waiting for me to slide myself into it, was taking deep breaths and holding them, so that when a horn honked as it went by, I about jumped out of my skin.

"You all right?" Camille asked, watching me from across the truck.

"Yeah," I said. "Just claustrophobic is all."

I took another deep breath and thought of my mom's letter, tucked snug in my jacket pocket right up against my heart.

The hardest thing to do is usually the right thing to do.

If I was going to do this thing, I might as well fucking do it right. There was no time to be a pussy.

Chapter Thirty-One

We stood in the kitchen. The lights were off and outside the sky was turning a velvety midnight blue. Crime scene tape marked an X across the basement entrance, the black hole of it fucking grinning as it waited.

"Yeah. I'm here, asshole," I said. Camille shot me a frown. I bounced on the balls of my feet and bobbed my head, pumping myself up. "Let's fucking do this."

I took a deep breath, took a hand off the dynamite to rip down the tape, and then went for the light switch.

"Ahhhhh!" I yelled as I flipped it up. War cry, you know?

"God, you're a dork," Camille said.

We looked down the stairs together and, god the vibe was so much worse with the lights on.

The harsh brightness bounced off the white-painted walls and glared onto the cement floor. Onto the blood stains, onto the chalk outline, onto the coiled rope.

We walked down the steps into the stillness, a stillness that felt like the inside of a dead person's brain, their last memory frozen in time like a stage with the lights left on after the show was over. Except now we were there, new actors being directed by someone in the shadows, saying lines we never rehearsed at the whim of the void that consumed everything. By the time we got to the bottom and I looked back up at the dark doorway, I wasn't even sure if there was anything on the other side anymore.

But with my nerves gone, I felt nothing at all. Not after seeing the proof of Denny's last night.

The feeling that I'd always been there, in that moment, came over me. As if it was there, in that basement, where I had listened to the prison humming through the night. That after seeing Shane tweak out under trailer I'd gone there, to the basement, and laid my head down. That, if I looked under the stairs, I'd find Nana's body stored away like some prop pulled from the theater.

It had all happened there.

Because whatever dark and unnatural force existed in Stewartville also existed in me. It *was* me. It was what sat heavy at the bottom of my soul, and I carried it with me wherever I went.

"Holy cow," Camille whispered as she came down the last step behind me. I'd almost forgotten she was there. "This place is creepy as fuck."

We dumped the bundles of dynamite on Denny's bed, right under his Richard Pryor posters, and went through his shit until we found a black bag to carry the dynamite.

"We need to move the entertainment stand," I told her. "The tunnel is behind there."

Once it was off the wall, I hitched the bag up on my shoulder and gave her a flashlight from the two that were waiting upright on the coffee table, right where Denny and I had left them.

She turned it on, bent down, and stepped through the hole. With a deep breath, I tossed the bag in and followed her.

Her flashlight swung left and right, up and down. "*Wow*," she breathed. "This is crazy."

"Pretty wild, huh?"

I crouched in front of the bag and unzipped it. "So, I'm gonna blow the entrance here," I said.

She gave me a look. "Is this really safe?" she asked. "Why don't we just explore and see if anything is even down here first?"

"It's safe," I hoped. "There's a turn up ahead. As long as we get around that…" I didn't say *then we shouldn't blow up*.

But she got my point. "Yeah. Okay."

"Why don't you wait there."

She nodded and left. I listened to her footsteps echoing against the stone walls, as I balanced a stick of dynamite on the ledge of the hole.

"Here," she called.

"Okay."

I took the fuses in my hand and sat back on my heels, looking into the basement one last time, picturing Denny and I on the empty couch, playing Mortal Kombat and joking about bullshit. Wishing his mom had never thrown that damn shoe.

I pushed myself up, put the bag over my shoulder, and walked backwards with the fuses, feeling like everything in that basement and everything in the world beyond it was what was really at the end of the tunnel. Like a box that existed in a vacuum of darkness. A sock inside out. And I was finally crawling out of it. Turning the sock right side in.

"Ready?" I called over my shoulder, lighter in position.

"Ready."

There was no going back now. I flicked the flame.

Smoke filled the tunnel. I dropped the fuses and hauled ass, skidding and tripping around the bend, smoke filling my lungs. I got around the corner, passing Denny's ripped down board, and kept on going. Camille ran along beside me until,

Boom!

Rocks flew past the bend and clattered against the walls and a cloud of dust spilled in all around us. Car alarms went off above our heads, muffled by earth and stone.

We coughed and waved the air in front of our faces and then I headed back to the bend. The beam of the flashlight cut through the dust around the corner and as it settled, I saw what I needed to see. Denny's basement was gone. Buried behind a wall of rock.

Buried just like Denny himself. I wiped my eyes and felt a weight lift from my shoulders.

"Rest in peace, man."

Chapter Thirty-Two

I met up with Camille, who was bent over dusting her tights off.

"Well. We're alive," she said, smirking up at me.

I lit a cigarette, feeling a little like a badass, and so I said, "Let's finish the fucker off," and took another drag like I was Arnold Schwarzenegger.

She took my hand in hers and we took a step together, and another, and then more and more, as we chased the dark circle of shadows ahead.

I tried to map our position, what street we'd be on up top, as we followed the tunnel around another bend north and then another east. I figured that much out at least and knew it was only the length of a cigarette to walk from Denny's to the edge of town.

A cockroach scurried along the wall past us and with it came the smell of cucumber. I looked up at the ceiling and thought about the hidden, dark spaces between baseboards and kitchen cabinets. Of peanut butter on mouse traps, of fish on hooks. Of Venus fly traps and borax. I took a deep breath and reached my hand into my pocket.

"My mom told me once that these tunnels were actually used by the miners," I said.

"Really?" Camille asked, waving her flashlight around as our footsteps echoed through the tunnel. From somewhere down the way came the sound of dripping water.

"Yeah," I said. "She said it was so they could run liquor and guns up to the Golden Faire without the union men seeing." I held the pack out to her. "Want one?"

She slid a smoke out of the box and I flicked the lighter and held it up for her. Her cheeks sucked in and the cherry flared.

She inhaled, French, the smoke pouring out her mouth and back into her nostrils.

I opened my hand and showed her the baggie. "But you knew that already, didn't you? Why are you doing it, Camille?"

She frowned and ran a hand through her red hair. "Dude, what are you being weird about *now*?"

"I found this baggie in Shane's truck." I gave her a minute, but she didn't reply so I pushed on. "It has strawberries on it."

"So?"

"These are the same baggies Roy used when he was dealing."

She took a drag, started walking again, still not looking at me. "So what?"

I followed and looked at the wall closest to me, just as she studied the wall closest to her. "Well, Roy's *dead*, Camille. So, who the fuck is dealing his shit now?"

She stopped and looked at me like I was an idiot. "Wait. You think it's *me?*"

I pulled Gavin's silver pentagram necklace from my pocket and held it up to her. "I found this in your room."

It dangled in the beam of our lights, dust sifting around it.

"You know, it took me a minute to put two and two together. But then I remembered you were with Mr. Anders that night at that motel. I'd thought you'd just been whoring it up, but really, you were selling him something much, much worse, weren't you?"

She glared at me, cheeks red.

"Not to mention the fact that Steve was with Zeke earlier today. Probably offered him a bump. A little something to lift his spirits. And Zeke, like everyone else on the shit, flipped the fuck out on it, didn't he?

And I'm guessing that's probably what happened to Berm, too."

But not Denny, a tiny voice reminded me. I shoved the thought back.

Camille's lips were little white lines now. She shook her head and started walking away, arms crossed. She had no choice, she couldn't turn back.

"Then I realized you were storing it down here." I said, following her and pushing her buttons. "Gavin knew and was trying to find a way in. So you got him high and I guess he drowned trying to kill his sister in the pool."

She ignored me so I asked again. "*Why*, Camille?"

She spun around to face me. "Because *fuck this town*, is why," she said. Tears welled up in her eyes and she crossed her arms over her chest. "Fuck this place and all the people in it."

A thin, black line of mascara coursed down her cheeks. She wiped it away and looked at me. "Because of what it did to Roy."

But I didn't have room for pity. Not now. Not here. I grabbed her elbow and yanked her towards me. "And getting Shane hooked? Was that just to get back at my mom, too?"

"*Me* getting back at your mom? Dude. That was *her* getting back at *you.*"

"What?"

"Oh, ho, ho. Something you *don't* know, Mr. Fucking Smart-ass. I told you, she was Roy's supplier. His connection. Did you really think she stopped just because she was locked up? Are you *kidding*? Business is even *better* for her now."

The truth of it hit me like a ton of bricks. A wall of bricks. And how easy it must have been to get to Shane, too, what with how fucking miserable he was.

I let go of Camille, not that I needed to hold on to her anymore. She got right up in my face all on her own. "Why don't you also take a guess at who had Zeke's mom jumped?"

I stared at her, a lump rising in my throat.

"That's right, asshole. Cheryl found out your fucking bitch of a mother wasn't actually all about that Christian, rehabilitation, friendship bracelet life. That she hadn't fucking changed at all." She shrugged and crossed her arms. "So, your mom shut her the fuck up."

I stared at my hand as it moved all on its own for my pocket, felt it grab the bracelet and pull it out, and then I stared at that too.

"Oh no," Camille laughed, harsh and bitter from somewhere far, far away. "Don't tell me she had you believing that shit, too."

Chapter Thirty-Three

The tunnel closed in on me. The walls pulsing and shifting in tighter. The shadows moving ever closer, but never quite touching me.

"I'm fucking out of here," she said.

I listened to her footsteps crunch on the gravel and echo on the stones until I found my voice.

"Camille."

She looked back, and I dropped my eyes, wishing she hadn't become such a fucking mess, wishing that we could go back to her place again, watch *DuckTales* like we used to, and eat those omelets we'd learned to make together in Home Ec.

"It got to you," I said.

She frowned. "What?"

"The curse of Stewartville. The thing you said turns us into our worst fears. It got to you."

"There is no *thing*, dummy. I was just fucking around with you because you were finally talking to me again."

I shook my head and chose my words carefully. "No. There *is* something about this place. Maybe not some monster or ghost, but something that locks us all in a prison and keeps us chained to the sins and mistakes of the past. Something that runs through the veins of this town and infects us." I raised my eyes and met hers, knowing I was playing a dangerous game. "And it turned you into her, Camille."

Her eyes widened slightly, and I took a step closer. She took a step back.

"Is that why you brought me down here," she asked, her bottom lip quivering. "To blow me up and rid the town of its demon?"

I stopped and frowned. "*What?* No." I ran a hand through my hair. "Jesus Christ. I don't want to *kill* you, Camille. I wanna blow up your stash."

She wrapped her arms around herself and a tear rolled down her cheek as she looked away. I took another step towards her.

"I promise, I'm not gonna hurt you, Camille. *You* wanted to come with *me*, remember? Why?"

She snapped her head back at me, her face pinched in anger. "I'd deserve it, you know," she spat. The tears were coming faster now, and she bounced on her feet with the emotion. "Some fucking lady over in Grand ate her kids on this shit. Zeke… Zeke…" and then she was sobbing.

"Shit," I whispered. I took another step, close enough to touch her. "You came because you want to end it too, don't you?"

She nodded and wept and I pulled her close to me. "I hate this place so much," she whispered.

"All right then," I said. "Let's go blow it up."

She wiped her eyes and pulled away. "You don't hate me?"

I flicked my cigarette away. "No, I don't hate you. You're a goddamn mess and probably a sociopath, but I don't hate you. We've all done horrible shit we regret, Camille."

She nodded. "Yeah. Okay. Let's blow it up."

We smiled at each other and then she took my hand again and led me through the tunnel and I followed, chewing on my thoughts a bit.

"Why did you really get involved with this, Camille?" I asked after a bit.

She sighed. "I don't know. I guess…" She stopped walking and looked at me. "Aren't you ever curious about how bad it can really get? Don't you ever get tired of waiting for that other shoe to drop, worried about who you'll become when it does? Worried about how well you'll survive it? I guess I just wanted to get it over with."

My whole life I'd been waiting. Waiting to see where I'd end up at the crossroad. So, I nodded.

A few minutes later, we came up to a wall with a board blocking the way through. Just like what Denny had found.

I went to move it out of the way and that's when I heard the scratching. I drew my hand back and looked at Camille.

"Something's back there," I whispered. "This is it."

Chapter Thirty-Four

I shined the light in and my heart sank.

"Come on in," Steve said.

I stepped through the hole and dropped the bag. As I wiped my hands on my jeans, I looked around the room. It was lit by a single bulb, an open walkway at one end, and white powder wrapped into bricks stacked against the left wall.

Camille climbed in behind me and went to stand beside Steve.

He bent down, grabbed a brick, and set it in the bag at his feet.

I lifted my eyes to Camille.

"So this is why you wanted to come with me?" I asked.

She bit her lip.

I nodded slowly and took it all in.

"It fucking stinks in here," I said finally.

Steve didn't answer.

"It's the landfill," Camille said, looking up at Steve like she might have done something wrong by talking.

So, we *were* somewhere close to the school. "When did you call him?"

"At the liquor store," Steve said.

I chuckled and crossed my arms. I'd gone from feeling like a bad ass to a dumb ass.

"So you found the boiler room entrance, I guess." I said.

"Well, it was stashed under your mom's trailer at first," Steve said. "But then we heard you guys talking about that dude Donny's —"

"Denny."

"— tunnel and decided that was so much fucking better."

I pictured Camille out on those porch steps, her hawk eyes watching us, and I busted out laughing.

"A fucking cat."

"What?" Steve asked.

If I didn't laugh, I'd cry. So, I just kept on cracking up. Cats and evil tunnels and moms, oh my.

Steve bent back down and grabbed another brick. "You're so fucking weird, dude."

I wiped my eyes. "So, let me guess, you were trying to clear it out before I blew it all to shit."

"Oh. We're still going to clear it out," Steve said, cracking his knuckles like a goon and stepping forward.

"No," I pulled the pistol from my waistband. "What you're gonna do is get the fuck out of here while I blow it all sky high."

Steve threw a look at Camille. "You didn't tell me he had a gun," he hissed.

That was interesting. Camille, the aspirin Queen.

I smiled. "Welp, asshole, I do."

He grinned. "You wouldn't —"

I pulled the trigger and Steve dropped to the ground. Camille screamed.

"Holy fuck!" Steve shouted over the ringing in my ears. His hands gripped his leg and blood seeped from between his fingers. "You fucking shot me, you crazy ass motherfucker!"

Holy shit was right. I'd seriously fucking shot him.

Camille bent down next to Steve and looked up at me with dark, wary eyes. "What the *fuck,* dude? What is wrong with you?"

"What's wrong with *me?*" I took a step forward and then caught myself. "Get him the fuck out of here," I told her. "Take him to the hospital."

They glanced at each other and she picked Steve up under his arms and backed up towards the exit, leaving a trail of blood behind them.

"I'm still blowing this place up," I called. Camille paused and looked up at me. "You'll want to get as far away as fucking possible as soon as you can."

She nodded and lifted Steve to his feet. He winced and cried out at the pressure on his leg.

"Hey!" I called. Camille looked over Steve's shoulder. "Denny didn't ever..."

She shook her head. "Not that I know of."

It was the last knife. I shouldn't have even asked.

"You should probably get out of here," I said, worn out and deflated.

"Are you —You're gonna be okay, right?"

"Who the fuck cares?" Steve snapped. "Fucker *shot* me, Camille."

"Yeah," I said, ignoring him. "I'll be fine."

She looked back at the table. "You don't really think I'm like her, do you?" she asked softly.

"You won't be," I said. "Not after this. Right?"

She nodded. They turned the corner, and I was alone.

After a few minutes, I pulled my headphones over my ears, lit a cigarette and unzipped the bag. One by one, I grabbed the sticks out and stuck them in among the bricks. When I grabbed the last two, my hand hit something else floating around the bottom of the bag.

I pulled out the tape and smiled.

Camille and her lowlife boyfriend needed some time to get clear, so I sat on the floor and put the tape in, then waited, spinning my lighter against the ground, and thinking about every fucked up thing that had happened. And how fucking funny it was that it had all led back to my goddamn mom. Not ley lines. Not vortexes. Not ghosts of schoolhouses past. Just my mom and her god damn drugs.

The light buzzed out and my Walkman died.

Chapter Thirty-Five

I tapped the button on the flashlight. Nothing. I hit rewind and play on the Walkman. Nothing.

"Come *on*," I hissed, pushing myself up. "Are you fucking kidding me?"

I let out a breath, my cheeks puffing out, and tried not to think of white spider fingers. I flicked my lighter and only got sparks.

"Yeah," I said to the darkness. "That just fucking figures."

I stuck a hand out and carefully shuffled forward. I flicked the lighter again. *Scratch, scratch* went the flint.

A child giggled, the sound of it bouncing towards me like a lonely, rolling ball.

I froze and listened closely for the sound of something more than dripping water.

"Hey, kid!"

The man's voice echoed down the tunnel.

"Hey! Where are you?" he called again. "I'm stuck back here."

I thought of those two little girls, throats slit in a little white house by the railroad tracks.

"Fuck off," I croaked. I cleared my throat and tried again. "Fuck off, asshole."

The man's laughter echoed toward me. "That's right, keep talking so I can find you. You're a real lifesaver, you know that?"

I scratched at the lighter again. A latch clicked somewhere and a door creaked open.

I held my breath.

"Denny! Shane! Denny!"

A chill went up my spine as Nana and Ms. Duncan screamed through the tunnel.

"Where's my head, you fat, fucking loser?"

I didn't bother with the lighter now. In the blackness came the sound of the thing shuffling towards me, pieces of its ground beef flesh hitting the cement with a squish and a splat.

I dropped to the ground and closed my eyes. I couldn't look at it. I'd see a face rearranged upon its bashed in skull, dropping scraps of brain like chum.

And if it saw me, if those hanging eyeballs fell on me, it would all be over. It would suck every bit of sanity out of me.

"You promised you fat, fucking good for nothing!" the Nana-Duncan monster screamed, so close now.

It banged against the walls and I jumped. Over and over and over it banged, and I covered my head with my hands and squeezed my eyes shut. Even if it touched me, I'd never open my eyes.

Then it stopped.

I waited for a good long while in the silence before lifting my head.

Someone sobbed in the darkness.

"They're here," a man whispered. I held my breath again and didn't move.

"They're in the bricks and stones," he said.

And then he giggled. A crazy, lunatic giggle.

The flashlight flickered on.

"Sweetie."

I dragged my tired eyes upward and looked at the tulpa. Shadows waved and pulsed around her as she smiled and opened the gate of the dog kennel. I was three years old again, and she was fifteen feet tall. Blonde hair teased and feathered. Blue eyeshadow and black mascara. She was wearing her jeans and cowboy boots, along with the necklace I'd made her from macaroni.

"Mommy has friends coming over. It's time to get in the kennel now," she said.

Fear choked my heart, strangled it in a slimy, cold grip.

"Be a good boy and get in," she coaxed.

"You're not real," I said to the room, sounding just like everyone in every horror movie ever made. Funny how things like that stick with you.

The light flickered once more.

"Sure I am, sweetie. Come on, now. You know what happens to bad boys."

The shadows crawled out of the kennel, moved in and out of the bricks, lapped at my feet. I stared into the cage and the blackness grew deeper, sucking the cell into it millimeter by millimeter. There was something down there. Something I desperately wanted to see. Something that tickled the edges of my brain.

I slid my back up the wall, standing, knowing that the minute I crawled in, the minute she shut the cage door, I'd be lost. Forever. Stuck in the vortex of weird.

"No," I said.

Her face changed, and she became the Terrible Mother. "I said get in the *fucking* kennel."

I shook my head, even as my shadow lengthened, drawing closer to that black hole.

"What the *fuck* are you waiting for?" she screeched, filling the tunnel with her rage. "Get inside before I beat your little, retarded ass."

Shadows waved and pulsed around me. Claustrophobia, my old familiar friend, gripped at my heart as they crawled out of the walls, moved in and out of the bricks, lapped at my feet.

"OK," I said. "This is it. I'm here now and I probably won't get out. But neither will you."

I scooted closer to the dynamite, the shadows scooting with me. I turned my head and called over my shoulder.

"Camille? You gone?"

The dark silence waited for an answer with me. With a prayer I flicked the lighter one last time.

It caught.

"This is for Denny and Zeke and Nana," I whispered.

I brought the flame forward with a grin.

"*Fatality*, motherfucker."

The fuses sparkled.

Smoke filled the room as I turned and ran for the exit. I tripped around the corner, fell forward on my hands, then pushed myself back up and sprinted as fast as I could through the blackness, hoping to God that I wasn't about to run face first into a wall.

The first explosion went off just as the Walkman clicked back on and the music filled my ears. The blast knocked me off my feet and as I lay there panting and listening to Johnny Cash, there was another blast and then another. Then the whole fucking earth rumbled and roared and opened up like I'd just unleashed hell.

Then they were coming. In the growing flames and falling rubble, the figures in the tunnel moved towards me, screaming and wailing and gnashing their teeth for my soul.

I pushed myself up, hurt and broken, and pulled out my pistol. I fired, fired again. I fired until I was out of bullets, as the heat rushed by me and the ghosts screamed, as the falling bricks threatened to bash me in the skull. And then one connected and it was lights out for me.

See, when I lit those fuses under the boiler room, I hadn't known there was also a pocket of methane trapped in that old landfill.

Bye-bye, Stewartville High.

From what I heard, the fireball roared up through the night and shook the whole damn town, letting car alarms off throughout the streets and knocking out a transformer or two. Generators kicked on at the prisons, but those few seconds of darkness were still enough to set off a mob that turned into a full-on riot by morning.

They pulled me out of the rubble about twelve hours later and I woke up two weeks after that, handcuffed to a hospital bed.

I'd slept through the worst of it, but after being drilled by the police for hours, I was emotionally dying for a smoke.

Thank god some high schooler went by my door. "Hey! Hey you!" I called.

He backed up and peeped in. I lifted my hand and pointed. "Can you hand me the remote?"

A cop popped his head around. "Shut up," he said to me. "Get going," to the kid.

"I just want a smoke!" I called after him, and just as it clicked with me who I sounded like, I got a glimpse of him rolling by in a wheelchair, his silver stubble catching the overhead light.

Then, when I was well enough, they transferred me over to the County Jail. I'd had my birthday while I was under. Happy eighteenth.

One of mom's crew had told me once that if I wanted to survive lock up, I needed to convince people I was crazy. Luckily, there wasn't any need for that. I was public enemy number one. The kid who had gone nuts, shot a classmate, and blown up the high school.

So, I got fingerprinted, got my asshole searched, got the lice shampoo treatment, the whole nine yards. They kept me in solitary for a while, just for evaluations, but after a bit I wound up sharing a cell with a guy named Mick. He'd just meant to pass through town but had wound up finding some trouble and staying long term. Isn't that just the way it goes?

I stayed at County until my sentencing came in (Guilty as sin, Your Honor). Then they loaded me up into the DOC bus and headed for Old Max.

Forehead pressed against the mesh wired windows, I looked for any signs that things had gotten better. That Stewartville was different somehow.

But litter still tumbled down the median, catching in the overgrown weeds where inmates were hard at work. The market was still as faded as ever, with a new board up in its window to cover the hole where a pane had shattered. Robbery. I knew because they had admitted the guy to County the night before. The stores were still empty, the glass in the windows still smeared. Dirt yards and broken-down cars still flew by as we rumbled down the road.

But change takes time, right? I laid my head back on the cracked plastic seat and let out a breath, and when we stopped at a light, I looked over and saw Shane's truck.

He was beating his head to music, tapping his hand on the wheel. He looked good.

"Hey!" I yelled through the shut window, hitting my hands against the wire. "Hey, Shane! Over here!"

"Knock it off, inmate!" a guard hollered. The light changed and with it Shane disappeared.

A few minutes later, we pulled off the highway onto Main and stopped in front of the prison gates. As I stared at the Golden Faire — lost in memories of nights spent at Comet's playing hacky sack and drinking beer — the gate guard hit the buzzer and called over his walkie-talkie to the reception tower.

"They're coming."

I chuckled at that — who wouldn't? — and looked down at my shackled hands, thinking of a frizzy-haired old man I'd known once.

After bending over and spreading my ass cheeks for one more round of searches, the door to the cell block buzzed open, and I started my slow, shuffling walk into a prison where I'd spend the rest of my life.

I had made it to the crossroads, and I'd taken a left instead of a right, after all. But I hadn't gone quietly. I'd defeated the evil of Stewartville and won.

Chapter Thirty-Six

"And that's why I'm here. The end."

"I don't know, man," Shep said when I finished my story. He'd stolen a case of Pabst and was in for two years.

I leaned against the bars and dangled my arms out. "What do you mean, *you don't know?*"

He went over to the toilet, pulled his khakis down, and squatted.

"Say all that's true. Then how come it didn't get to you?"

"What do you mean?"

"Well, every time you tell this story, I've been meaning to ask: What was your worst fear?"

I frowned.

"Yeah, boy, tell us," Lawrence called from the next cell over.

An alarm buzzed.

"Lights out," the guard called. His keys jangled down the hall as he made checks and then the overheads went out, replaced by an orange glow that washed over the cell. I went over to the cot, chest tight, and laid down.

"Face facts, man," Lawrence said again. "This place got to you. They done locked you up and throwed away the key. You ain't never getting out."

"Leave the kid alone," Shep said, standing to wipe his ass.

"Hell no. Crazy ass mother fucker blew up a school and shot four people."

I swallowed and looked at the pictures glued with toothpaste to the bottom of the top bunk. Shane had sold the trailer, had left town, had gone to State.

"You got it all wrong," I said. "I'm a hero." But something about Shep's words gnawed at my brain until I fell asleep.

Two days later I looked up from my cot as the library book cart came to a squeaking stop in front of my cell.

"Here's that stuff you wanted," Barney said, sticking a Ziploc baggie through the bars. His wrinkled face looked over his bony shoulder back down the hall. "Don't tell anyone I gave it to you, dough."

I rose, trying to keep myself calm, and grabbed it from him as casually as possible. "Thanks, man."

"Took me forever to find that," he said. "Was buried away in some storage box. Almost got caught by Willoughby."

"Appreciate it."

I went back to the cot, opened the bag, and held the book in my hands. *Mr. Snuffle's Bone*

I smiled, put the tape in the recorder, and pushed play.

It'd been four years since Denny and I had made that tape and listening to us after all that time, just being stupid kids laughing and joking, brought tears to my eyes. Damn, it was good to hear his voice again.

When the story ended, I waited through the dead air for the skit to begin.

"Hey, did —?"

"Greetings, Prisoners of Stewartville—"

I frowned and stopped the tape. I hit rewind, held the recorder up to my ear, then hit play again.

Whispering.

"Hey, did you —?"

"Greetings, Prisoners of Stewartville—"

Stop, rewind, play.

burn it Casey burn it burn it Casey burn it

"Hey, did you —"

"Greetings, Prisoners of Stewartville —"

The recorder clattered open as it hit the cement floor and the cell walls closed in on me, claustrophobia tightening chest.

It makes people become their worst fear.

"No-no-no." I said, backing up.

What happens if it gets to the wrong person?

"No!" I shouted, spinning round, trying to make sense of it. "No! No!"

That prison gives it plenty of negative energy to feed on. Like pigs in a pen.

I ran to the bars and shook them.

"*Hey!*" I screamed. "*Please!* I shouldn't be here. *Help!*"

Laughter came down the dim hallway until all the cells but two were cackling with it. And the shadows in the walls just drew closer.

What if it gets someone to Donald Geist the place?

I slid to the floor. It was me. All along it was me. And I was never getting out.

There is something about this place. Something that locks us all in a prison, chained to the sins and mistakes of the past.

"Please," I begged, my face pressed against the bars, tears rolling down my cheeks. "I'm sorry. *Please.*" And then I heard it.

Scratching in the walls.

About the Author

Shannon Felton lives in Buckeye, Arizona with her husband, their four children, and three dogs. This is her debut novella.

Acknowledgements

Special Thanks to Meredith Lozaga and Kim Arntsen, as well as the amazing writers of RDR, for the incredible help and support they provided.

More From Brigids Gate Press

Coming September 2022

During the Spring Equinox underneath London, four people enter the caves, but only one will survive. Each trespasser must battle their own demons before facing the White Lady who rises each year to feed on human flesh.

Available now

A terrifying pandemic sweeps the world, rendering its victims completely immobile but leaving them conscious with their minds intact. The victims are helpless against the environment, completely at the mercy of wild animals, weather, out of control fires, and other dangers. There's no hope for those safe in their homes either, as they slowly starve to death, unable to feed themselves or drink.

Dr. Alex Griffiths leads a team racing against time to find a cure before it's too late. Will he succeed?

Available now

Decades after his grandfather was buried alive in a Californian gold mine, Dr. Nick Jones teams up with an adventure travel influencer to venture underground and film a documentary, telling the story of what really happened.

What should be a dream come true soon becomes a nightmare as someone or something stirs…BELOW.

Coming August 2022

On the run from a life of prostitution and poverty, exotic dancer Cece Dulac agrees to become the main attraction at an erotic séance hosted by an enigmatic mesmerist, Monsieur Rossignol. As the séance descends into depravity, Cece falls prey to Rossignol's hypnotic power and becomes possessed by a malevolent spirit.

George Dashwood, an aspiring artist, witnesses the séance and fears for Cece. He seeks her out and she seduces him, but she is no longer herself. The spirit controlling her forces her to commit increasingly depraved acts. When the spirit's desire for revenge escalates to murder, George and Cece must find a way to break Rossignol's spell before Cece's soul is condemned forever.

Marionette is an erotic horror novella inspired by traditional folk tales and set in fin de siècle Paris.